TOINETTE'S PHILIP

MRS. C. V. JAMISON

Published by Left of Brain Books

Copyright © 2021 Left of Brain Books

ISBN 978-1-396-32204-4

First Edition

Table of Contents

CHAPTER I

PHILIP, DEA, AND HOMO

ONE sunny morning early in March, two children, a boy and a girl, followed by a large shaggy dog, slowly sauntered up Rue Royale, in the French quarter of New Orleans. The boy was about nine years old, the girl not more than eight, the dog—no one could tell his age with any degree of certainty; but he was no longer young, for the gray hairs about his muzzle and his long hollow flanks plainly showed that he had seen many and evil days. He was of the breed commonly called "wolf," his body was covered with coarse, bristling hair, and his long nose and pointed, alert ears gave him an intelligent and inquisitive look in spite of his drooping tail and spiritless walk. Without looking to the right or left he followed closely on the heels of the children, occasionally sniffing at a bag which hung over the boy's shoulder. When they slackened their pace to glance into a shop-window or to make room for a passer, the dog also stopped, while he eyed the bag wistfully, a few drops of water now and then falling from his mouth on the pavement.

The boy, from time to time, glanced down at the patient creature, smiling while he reached out a thin brown hand to pat his head fondly.

"Homo smells my lunch. It's no use, I must stop and give him some," he said at last, placing on a door-step near him a tray of flowers which he was carefully carrying.

He was a handsome boy, lithe and slim, and tall for his age, with large blue eyes of a merry cast, straight clear features, and curling brown hair. He was cleanly but poorly clad in a blue shirt, and short trousers of the same color; a small white cap covered a portion of his thick hair, which lay in heavy rings over his forehead just above his straight dark eyebrows. The little girl who accompanied him was an uncommon and picturesque figure. A dark red frock fell straight to her heels, a white muslin scarf crossed in front was tied behind, the long ends almost touching the pavement when she walked, her very thick black hair was cut off square, like a mane over her shoulders, and it was partly covered by a red silk kerchief knotted under her chin, her little worn prematurely old face was as white and delicate as a Roman cameo, her eyes, unnaturally large, were intensely dark—so dark that they showed through her drooping lids, and her small firmly closed mouth seemed never to have smiled. On her arm she carried a basket, in which, carefully packed in soft paper, were several little colored wax figures delicately and beautifully modeled. One was "Esmeralda and her goat"; another, "Dea and the wolf"; another, "Quasimodo,"—in short they all represented characters taken from the stories of Victor Hugo. That they were of almost sacred value to the child was apparent in the careful way she carried them, and the occasional glance of pride and solicitude she bestowed upon them.

PHILIP, DEA, AND "HOMO."

When the boy stopped and put down his tray of flowers, orange-blossoms, roses and violets, she too stopped and placed her basket on the steps, drawing,

as she did so, a thick paper over the little figures to shield them from the sun and dust.

After the boy's hands were free he proceeded to unfasten the bag, smiling all the time at the old dog who pressed close to him, his sunken eyes full of expectation.

"Don't be in a hurry, Homo; don't be in a hurry," he said, gently. "You shall have your breakfast. I made Mammy Toinette put in plenty of bread. I knew you'd be hungry; I knew you would."

The little girl, with her hands tightly clasped, stood looking on almost as anxiously as the dog. Suddenly the boy fixed his eyes on her inquiringly, and his face flushed to his forehead.

"Did you have anything to eat before you came out, Dea—now tell me the truth, did you?" he asked, earnestly.

The child turned paler, if possible, and looked away evasively, but made no reply.

"Tell me now, Dea, quick! I sha'n't give Homo a mouthful till you tell me."

"I didn't want anything to eat, Philip," she said, tremulously. "*Pauv'* papa had one of his bad spells."

"And you didn't sleep any last night. I can tell by your looks that you didn't."

"Not much," she replied, sighing. "*Pauv'* papa walked all night. I think he was in pain. I couldn't sleep when he was suffering."

"You couldn't, of course," said the boy, soothingly. "But never mind now, Dea—eat some breakfast and give Homo some. You like Mammy's fried chicken—and I've enough for all of us."

And as the boy spoke he unfolded a clean white napkin and displayed some squares of corn bread and a quantity of chicken fried crisp and brown. "Take all you want"—and he held it out invitingly.

"I'll give some to Homo," said the girl, taking a piece of the chicken with the tips of her slender fingers and offering it to the old dog, who swallowed it without the least attempt to chew it, sighing contentedly as it did so.

While the girl and the dog were eating, the boy uncovered the basket, and taking out one by one the small figures, looked at them admiringly, turning them to blow off an occasional speck of dust.

"They're as natural as life, Dea," he said, encouragingly. "I hope you'll sell one to-day. You haven't sold one since Mardi Gras, have you? It must be the rainy weather that has kept people out of the streets; but now it's cleared off Rue Royale will be full of strangers, and you'll be sure to sell one to-day."

"Oh, I hope so, Philip, for *pauv'* papa's sake," replied the girl as she gave her last crumb of bread to the dog. "He hasn't any money, and he's so unhappy when he hasn't any money." Then she covered her face with her hands and began to cry silently.

"Don't, Dea, don't cry," said the boy gently, as he took up his tray of flowers and the child's basket as well. "Come on, let's hurry. Grande Seline will be back to-day, and she's sure to bring you something."

"But if she *isn't* there, Philip, what shall I do? *Pauv'* papa had no supper last night, and there's no breakfast for him this morning. I ought to have taken him the bread and chicken you gave me. Homo and I could have waited. I wasn't so hungry, because I had your lunch yesterday. Now it's gone; we have eaten it, and *pauv'* papa hasn't any."

"Take the rest of my lunch, Dea," said the boy, stoutly. "I don't want it, I can wait till night. Mammy Toinette promised me gumbo for supper."

The little girl smiled faintly through her tears as she trotted on beside her friend, who still carried her basket. "Gumbo! how nice to have gumbo for supper!" she said, with a soft sigh.

"Yes, it's good with plenty of rice," replied her companion; "and Mammy would give you some if you'd go home with me."

"I can't, Philip. Papa would be angry; he never allows me to go into any house, and he never has any one to visit him."

"That's why he has no money and doesn't sell more little images," returned the boy, with some show of anger. "If he made friends, you would not have to go hungry."

"*Pauv'* papa," sighed the child, "he's so ill and unhappy. He cried when he put Quasimodo in the basket; he said it was the best figure he had ever modeled—that it was a work of art, and worth a great deal."

"A work of art," repeated the boy, scornfully. "It's not half as pretty as Esmeralda and her goat. It's an ugly, crooked little monster."

"Well, Quasimodo was like that," returned Dea, with some spirit. "Papa has often read to me about him: he was *carillonneur* of Notre Dame de Paris."

"Oh, yes, I know. You've told me all about him, don't you remember? But I like Esmeralda best. I'm sure you'll sell Esmeralda first."

"I hope so; *pauv'* papa said I *must* sell something to-day. If I don't, Philip, I'm sure he will walk again to-night."

"Well, let's hurry then," cried Philip, quickening his steps. "If Grande Seline is there, she'll help us to find a customer; and she promised to be there to-day."

CHAPTER II

GRANDE SELINE

"OH, there's Grande Seline!" cried Philip, joyfully, as they drew near the old Union Bank, not far from Canal street. "She's setting up her stand now."

"Yes, there she is!" exclaimed Dea, starting into a swift run toward a stout laughing mulattress, who was standing near a table under the portico of the Bank, tying a white apron around her thick waist.

"Oh, honey," she gurgled as she clasped the child tight. "Oh, honey, how glad I is ter see yer—an' Mars' Philip, too!—how you's both done growed since I's been gone."

"And how thin you've got, Seline," returned Philip, his blue eyes sparkling with merriment. "You've lost flesh going to the country to your cousin's wedding."

"My, my, jes' hear dat boy! Do yer think I's slimmer, Ma'mselle Dea?" and she looked complacently at her fat sides as she smoothed the folds of her starched apron. "An' what's you chil'run been er-doin' all dis yere time dat I's been away? An' how's yer *pauv'* papa, Ma'mselle?"

"He's very bad, Seline; he don't sleep," returned Dea, sighing sadly.

"My, my, honey, I's sorry ter hear sech bad newses," said Seline, with sympathy. "An' is yer done sole any yer little images while I 's gone ter der weddin'?"

"No, Seline, not one. *Pauv'* papa's finished Quasimodo. I've got him in my basket; I'm to sell him for five dollars."

"Well, honey, ef yer want ter sell him yer got ter stan' him out where people'll see him; 't ain't no use ter keep him covered up in yer basket. I'm goin' ter give yer a corner of my table," and Grande Seline swept aside her pile of fruits and cakes, smiling benevolently as she did so.

"But the dust, Seline!—papa doesn't like them to get dusty."

"Never mind der dust, chile; it'll blow off. It's der money we want, an' I don't see how yer goin' ter sell dat pore little crooked image," and Seline looked doubtfully at the work of art as Dea disencumbered it of its wrappings, and stood it as far away as possible from a generous pile of pralines. "Now, dat little one with the goat is right peart-lookin', an' it's strange yer don't sell it."

"You see, it's rained ever since you went away, Seline, and there's been no strangers in the streets," said Philip, coming forward to move Quasimodo a little more into the shadow of one of the fluted columns that decorate the façade of the old Bank. "If it hadn't been for funerals and weddings, Mammy wouldn't have sold any flowers. I've been here every day since you went to the country, and I haven't sold a dozen *boutonnières*."

"Dat's 'cause yer didn't have my table ter show yer flowers on, Mars' Philip. No one don't notice little creturs like you is. It takes an ole woman like I is ter get customers," said Grande Seline, chuckling and shaking her fat sides, as she arranged Philip's flowers and sprinkled them lightly from a can of water. "An' dat ole dog, too, he knows I's back; he's dun tuk his same place under dis yer table. Jes' look at the pore cretur; he's ter home, shore."

"Yes, Homo's glad you're back, Seline, and so are we," said Philip, leaning over the table and smiling up into the kind, dusky face. "I don't know which of us has missed you most, but I think Dea has."

"Pore chile," and the old woman glanced fondly at the little girl. "I's thought heaps about yer boaf, an' I's glad I's back. Yer ain't had yer scarf washed since I's gone, is yer, honey? Well, jes' slip it off when yer go home an' I'll bring it ter yer clean in der mornin'. An' see what I got in my basket fer yer supper ter-night," making a little pantomime to Philip as she took out a package folded in a clean napkin. "A half a chicken I done brought from the country, some flour bread, an' a slice of dat cheese yer *pauv'* papa likes; an' jes' look at dis yere, chil'run, some of der weddin'-cake fer yer. It's fine cake. Dat cousin knows how ter make cake; her ole Miss' learned her. Now ain't dat dar pretty cake as yer ever seed?"

"Oh, oh, Seline, isn't it nice!" cried both children at once,—"and the sugar on it is so thick and white."

"Now, you jes' eat some," she said, handing a generous slice to each; "an' dis what's left is part fer yer *pauv'* papa, Ma'mselle, an' part fer yer mammy, Mars' Philip."

"Why, Seline, you're awful good," cried the boy, his mouth full of cake. "I told Dea you'd bring us something from the country."

"May I keep half of mine for to-morrow, Seline?" asked Dea, when she had slowly eaten a part of hers.

"Why, yes, chile, if yer wants ter; an' jes' take dis yer bundle of chicken an' put it in der bottom of yer basket fer yer supper."

Dea took the package with trembling hands and glistening eyes. "Oh, Seline, how good you are! *Pauv'* papa will be so glad," she whispered.

"Yes, I knows, honey, I knows; an' I'm goin' ter sell one of dem little images fer yer papa dis yere day, er my name ain't Seline. I ain't been right yere in dis place since endurin' the war fer nothin'. My ole Mars' what was pres'dent of dis yer bank—yer see, chil'run, it use ter be a bank full of money afore der war—he done tole me I could set up my stan' yere; he say: 'Seline, you'll make yer fortune yere.' Well, I ain't made no fortune, but I 's done made right smart, an' now I 's got plenty to do a little fer you, honey, what ain't got no ma, only a *pauv'* sick papa, so I 's goin' ter help yer sell yer little images. Yer tired an' sleepy, chile; jes' drap down on my little stool an' take a nap in der shade, an' I'll look out for customers."

Dea did not wait for a second invitation to sleep. Her poor little head ached, and her eyes were heavy from her nights' vigils, so she sank down contentedly in Seline's broad shadow, and, resting her pale face against the good woman's clean apron, she slept as peacefully as did the old dog at her feet; and Philip, perched on the base of one of the massive columns, swung his bare brown legs and whistled softly, while he waited for the customer promised by Seline with so much confidence.

CHAPTER III

How They Became Acquainted

SOME ten or twelve years before the beginning of this story, when Grande
Seline had established her lunch-stand under the portico of the Union Bank, the
handsome structure was used for the purpose indicated by the name cut in large
letters on the stone façade; but the civil war and numerous unfortunate
financial changes had abolished the business, and the fine old building had
degenerated from its dignified position into a second-class theater or variety-
show. On the massive fluted columns hung huge colored posters and against
the gray old walls were fastened tall boards covered with ludicrous pictures of
dancing dogs, Chinese jugglers, and absurd caricatures, set forth in glaring
colors in order to attract the attention of the common people. Where formerly
grave, black-coated financiers passed in and out, now lounged a motley crowd
to read the playbills or scan the grotesque pictures, jesting and laughing as they
elbowed and jostled one another. Among them were some of the better class,
who lingered near Seline's stand in the corner of the portico to drink a glass of
her cold lemonade or to eat some of her fresh pralines, crisp and toothsome,
with the nuts showing thickly through their glossy coats. And beside her sweets,
in a clean basket carefully covered with a fresh napkin, were dainty sandwiches
of French rolls filled with chicken or ham, and the lightest and whitest of sponge
cake liberally coated with sugar. In the old days it was the custom of the busy
officials of the Bank to snatch a hasty lunch from Seline's basket, and to wash it
down with a glass of her delicious lemonade. Now it was another class that
patronized her; still the quality of her wares remained the same, therefore she
always had a large custom among the habitués of the theater, and in the course
of all these years she had saved up a snug little sum, and could well afford to be
generous at times.

Two or three years before, when Philip had first made his appearance on
Rue Royale with his tray of flowers, while lingering near her stand to feast his

eyes on her tempting display, Seline's attention was attracted by his innocent, charming face. He was not more than six years old at that time, and his merry laugh and pleasant chatter won her heart at once. From that day she took him under her especial care, and Philip's fresh, fragrant flowers always found a shady corner on Seline's table.

Not long after these friendly relations began, the boy appeared one day with a pale, sad-eyed little girl, dressed in a shabby black frock and carrying a small basket, in which were a few exquisitely modeled wax figures. He introduced his companion with great confidence to Grande Seline, taking it for granted that the kindly woman would extend to his forlorn little friend the affection she so freely lavished upon him. And he was not mistaken. Seline took the mournful little creature right to her great heart.

"I al'ays done loved little gals der best. Boys is good ernuff, but mighty triflin' and tryin'," she said by way of excuse to Philip, who she feared might be a little jealous of her sudden interest in Dea.

Philip first met the little girl on Ursulines street. She was in great trouble: an overfed bulldog had attacked Homo when he was very hungry, and consequently very weak, and though the poor old animal fought bravely, he was about to be "the under dog in the fight," when Philip appeared, and so sturdily belabored the enemy with a stout stick, that he let go and stood at bay, while Homo took refuge in instant flight, followed by the little girl, who, in her excitement, left her basket on the banquette. Philip, after he had driven the bulldog into a near yard and closed the gate upon him, picked up the neglected property and ran after the owner.

Poor little thing, she was frightened and breathless, but she stopped to thank her deliverer, between her sobs, while she grasped the dog's collar with both trembling hands.

"It wasn't Homo's fault," she explained, in rapid French. "The other dog began it. Homo's old and hungry, but he's got lots of spirit, and he won't bear an insult. The dog was rude to Homo, and he couldn't help fighting."

"I know," returned Philip. "I don't blame your dog; he couldn't help standing up to a saucy beast like that."

His ready sympathy, and sensible appreciation of Homo's self-respect, won the little girl's confidence at once, and from that day they were fast friends. She was very reticent, and Philip, with inborn delicacy, did not question her much; but from her remarks he learned that she lived on Villeré street, that her mother was dead, and that her father was an artist *en cire*, and that he modeled the pretty little figures which she tried to sell from house to house.

"*Pauv'* papa is always ill," she explained, in a grave, soft little voice. "His head hurts him, and he can't sleep at night; and since mama died he never sees any one, and never goes out in the day; he says the light hurts him. Sometimes he goes out in the evening and stays a long time. I don't know where he goes, but I think it is to the *cimetière*, to mama's grave."

Philip's bright face clouded; he felt like crying with the child, but he said bravely: "I wish you'd come with me up on Rue Royale; you'd have a better chance. I've a friend there who has a stand; her name is Grande Seline; she'll help you sell your little figures."

Dea gratefully accepted the kindly invitation, and having the good fortune to win Seline's affection at first sight, the child found a faithful friend, who cared for her in many ways with remarkable tenderness and devotion.

Every day, in rain or shine, the handsome boy and the sad-faced little girl could be found near Seline, while their wares occupied a part of her table, under which Homo slept soundly—a weary animal, who at last had found a secure and peaceful haven of rest.

The first break in this pleasant arrangement was when Seline went for a few weeks into the country to be present at the wedding of a dusky kinswoman. Now she had returned, much to the delight of the children, who entered upon their former relations with the utmost confidence and security.

CHAPTER IV

LILYBEL

POOR little Dea slept peacefully, safe under Seline's friendly shadow, and Philip whistled merrily now that his burden of care had fallen on broader and stronger shoulders; and while Dea slept, and Philip whistled, Seline drowsed in the soft spring air, slowly waving her bunch of peacock feathers to keep off the flies. This she did quite mechanically, whether her eyes were open or closed, and it served a good purpose in keeping pilfering fingers away from her sweets, as well as banishing the obtrusive winged creatures that hovered above her; for Seline was often in the land of dreams when her feathers were waving back and forth with rythmic precision.

On this day she slept with one eye open, for she was on the look-out for a suitable owner for Esmeralda or Quasimodo. "It's 'bout time fer strangers ter come erlong," she said to herself, "an' I knows er stranger soon's I set eyes on one; dey's der ones what buys dem little images."

Suddenly both eyes opened wide, and Seline straightened up and looked toward Canal street.

"Sure's I's born, dar's dat Lilybel er comin'. What dat boy er comin' yere dis time er day fur?—didn't I sont him on der levee, an' tole him ter stay dar till he done sole all what he got in his basket?"

Philip stopped whistling, and turned amused eyes toward Lilybel, who slowly approached, looking very sheepish. He was a mite of a darky, as black and glossy as a rubber shoe, with large whites to his bead-like eyes, and teeth that glistened like grains of new corn. His sunburned hair stood off from his head as though he were in a state of chronic fright, and his broad mouth was stretched almost from ear to ear in a mirth-provoking grin; his body was round and fat, and from his short, crooked legs his large feet stood out at right angles. One ragged suspender over a torn dirty shirt held up a muddy bundle of breeches, the ragged legs of which were rolled close to his thighs. Altogether he looked more like a small scarecrow than a member of the human family, and had it not been for his rolling eyes and broad grin, Lilybel would have deceived the wisest old crow in a corn-field.

"Now, jes' look at dat boy,—ain't he er sight?" cried Seline in a shrill voice, a voice cultivated expressly for Lilybel. "I done sont him out clean an' peart dis mornin', an' now yere he is, all muddy and frazzled. I suttenly knows he's er been rollin' down der levee with jes' sich triflin' chil'run like he self. Come yere," and she thrust out a threatening hand, which Lilybel adroitly dodged; "come yere, I say, afore I slap yer head off."

Lilybel paid no attention to his mother's startling threat, but skilfully kept out of reach, until he wormed himself behind the column where Philip sat laughing, in spite of Seline's trouble; and there, in an excellent position for dodging a stray shot, he looked out, grinning defiantly.

"Is yer goin' ter come yere," cried Seline, quite beside herself. "Jes' let me get my han' on yer," and she jumped up so suddenly that she dropped her bunch of feathers in her jar of lemonade, while she nearly overturned Dea, who awoke startled and confused at the fracas. And even Homo arose, alertly, and sniffed the air, then turned around and curled himself up for another nap. It was nothing—he was accustomed to these scenes between Lilybel and Seline. "Does yer hear me? Come yere an' tell me what yer done with yer basket," and leaning across the table in a frantic effort to grab the culprit, Seline came near sending Quasimodo to sudden and irreparable ruin, while she scattered a shower of pecans over the pavement.

Lilybel could not resist scrambling for some of the nuts, and while intent on his hunt, his mother caught him by the remnant of his shirt, and dragged him up before a terrible and pitiless tribunal.

Finding himself a prisoner beyond hope of escape, Lilybel, assuming an injured expression, declared with a mournful rolling of his eyes, "dat he hadn't done nofin', on'y jes' tumbled in der ruver an' got fished out when he was mos' drownded."

"An' whar's yer basket?—what yer done with yer basket?" cried Seline, shaking Lilybel so energetically that he looked like a bundle of tatters in a strong wind.

"It's done los' in der ruver," mumbled Lilybel, rolling his eyes and sniffling.

"LILYBEL COULD NOT RESIST SCRAMBLING FOR SOME OF THE NUTS, AND
SELINE CAUGHT HIM."

"Los' in der ruver," repeated Seline, slowly. "Now, chile, yer isn't tellin' der trufe, an' yer knows I won't have no boys a-tellin' me lies. I'll wear dat peach-tree switch out on yer dis night ef yer don't tell der trufe."

"It's der trufe, ma, es sure as I is a-stan'in' yere," returned Lilybel, stoutly. "I done los' it in der ruver."

"How cum yer los' it in der ruver?—tell me, how cum yer los' it dar?" and Seline emphasized her question with another shake, which made Lilybel's teeth chatter, while a shower of muddy water flew from his rags all over his mother's white apron.

"It's dis yere way I los' it," gasped Lilybel, hastening to explain. "I done went on er plank, whar dem rousterbouts is a wheelin' coal on a big steamer, an' jes' es I was er showin' my cakes, a big feller run inter me an' push me flop inter der ruver. An', ma, I was nearly drownded—I was nearly dade," cried Lilybel, growing pathetic, as he approached the climax; "I done cum up der las' time, when er rousterbout grab me an' pull me out."

"I won'er ef yer *is* er tellin' me der trufe, Lilybel?" questioned Seline, doubtfully, as she relaxed her grasp a little.

"I is, ma—I *is*," and Lilybel rolled his eyes and twisted his mouth into various affirmative contortions, while Seline held him at arm's-length and examined him critically.

"It's no use ter b'lieve yer, Lilybel. I jes' got ter fin' out ef yer did fall inter der ruver an' los' yer basket," continued Seline, solemnly; "but ef yer is er tellin' der trufe, yer suttenly didn't have *much* in yer basket when yer done los' it, 'cause yer is full almos' ter burstin' wid dem cakes an' pralines. Oh, yer is a triflin', worryin' chile, an' I has gotter use der rod on yer plenty 'fore I's done with yer. Go down dar an' curl up with dat ole dog. It's der best place fer yer," and with a sounding slap Seline thrust the culprit under the table, close to Homo, where, with a satisfied chuckle he nestled down, his head on the dog, and in a few moments was sleeping as soundly and irresponsibly as the animal beside him.

"Now, Mars' Philip, yer see what er trial I's got," said Seline, turning to Philip for sympathy. "It ain't no use puttin' conference in Lilybel. I 'spects he done eat dem cakes an' pralines, an' frowed dat basket erway. My, my, he's goin' ter ruin me ef I lets him have er basket. How cum dat boy's so bad?" continued Seline, reflectively. "An' I done name him fer his two little sisters what's dade—two peart chil'run as yer ever did see, an' jes' es sweet an' good es Ma'mselle Dea. It's jes' es I say: gals is na'chly good, an' boys is na'chly bad."

"Oh, Seline, I'm a boy," interposed Philip, "and I'm not so bad."

"No, no, honey, *yer* isn't bad; but yer white, an' white boys is different."

"Only think, Seline, Lilybel might have drowned," said Dea, softly; "then how sorry you would have been."

"Dat boy drownded!—no, no, chile. I's more feared he's born ter be hanged, 'cause Lilybel's mighty manish, an' trainin' don't do him no good. I's got heaps ef trouble with dat boy."

While this conversation was in progress, Seline tidied up her table, and restored Quasimodo to his original position, still intent, in spite of Lilybel's unexpected interruption, on finding a customer.

"Dar's dat stranger what useter pass yere right often fer flowers an' pralines. He's goin' ter buy yer little image if he comes ter day. He paints pictures up in der top of dat tall house down yere on Rue Royale, an' he's from der Norf, an' rich—rich."

Dea's little wan face took on a pleased, expectant look. Seating herself primly on the stool beside Seline, she watched the passers attentively, while Philip, standing on the edge of the banquette, whistled impatiently as he scanned the people on the opposite side of the street.

CHAPTER V

DEA SELLS QUASIMODO

THE painter from the North who was "rich—rich," as Seline said, had often stopped at her stand to buy a handful of pecans or a few of her crisp pralines, and as often as he came, he studied with the eye of an artist the two children who were always there, and many a dime found its way into Philip's pocket in return for a sprig of sweet-olive and a few violets.

It was true that he was a painter. His name was Edward Ainsworth, and he was an artist of some note in New York; but as to his being "rich—rich," Seline had only guessed it: first, because he was a stranger, and secondly, because he bought flowers nearly every day, and no one but a rich man would *buy* flowers.

On this day, Seline, full of anxious expectation, saw him approaching, and at first she thought he was about to pass, but no, he stopped suddenly, and swinging around, leaned over the table and buried his face in Philip's tray of odorous flowers.

"How fragrant! How delicious!" he said to himself in a low voice.

Then he selected a sprig of sweet-olive and a handful of violets, all the while looking from Philip to Dea, who stood with their large questioning eyes fixed on him.

In the mean time, Seline had put on her most genial smile, and when the customer laid down a dime for some pecans, she said in her smooth, rich voice, "They're fresh, right fresh, M'sieur; an' won't yer have a few pralines for lagnappe?"

"Certainly; thank you," replied the artist, still looking at the children, while he twisted the top of the little paper bag that contained his purchases.

"If yer please, M'sieur, I'd like ter show yer dis yere little image," and Seline gently introduced Quasimodo, while Dea turned paler, and Philip's eyes were full of anxiety. It was a moment of intense interest.

The artist's face brightened. He laid down the flowers and the paper bag, and taking the little figure almost reverently he turned and examined it critically. "Who made this?" he asked, looking from one to the other.

"My papa," said Dea, finding her courage and her voice at the same time.

"Your papa! Well, he is a genius. It is perfectly modeled. What is your papa's name, and where does he live?"

Dea dropped her head and made no reply. The artist looked inquiringly at Seline.

"Her *pauv'* papa is al'ays sick," said the woman, touching her forehead significantly; "he doesn't like to see no one. She," with a glance at Dea, "won't never tell strangers where she lives."

"Oh! I see," murmured the artist. "Well, my child," turning to the little girl and speaking very gently, "can you tell me what character this figure represents?"

"It is Quasimodo."

"Of course. It's perfect—perfect; but what a strange subject!" and again he turned it and examined it still more closely.

"Do you want to sell it?" he asked at length.

"Oh, yes, M'sieur," cried Dea, eagerly. "If you only will buy it, *pauv'* papa will be so glad,—he told me that I *must* sell it to-day."

"How much do you ask for it?"

"Papa said I could sell it for five dollars. Is five dollars too much?" faltered Dea. "He said it was a work of art, but if you think it is too much—"

"It *is* a work of art," interrupted the painter, as, with an absent-minded air, he introduced his thumb and finger into his waistcoat pocket and drew out a crisp note.

Dea's eyes sparkled and then grew dim with tears.

"But tell me, if you can, how long it took your father to model this?" he asked, still holding the note.

"Oh, a long time, M'sieur. I can't tell just how long, because he works at night when I'm asleep."

"Ah! he works at night,—and do you sell many?"

"No, M'sieur, I have not sold one for a long time."

"She hasn't sold one since Mardi Gras," interposed Philip with an air of great interest. "A stranger bought one then, but he only gave three dollars for it."

"Are you her brother?" asked the artist, smiling down at Philip.

"Oh, no, M'sieur, we're not related," replied the boy. "She's just my friend. She's a girl, and I try to take care of her, and help her all I can," and as the boy spoke he raised his eyes, and there was such a sweet light in their blue depths that the man's heart was touched with a very tender memory. "How much he is like him," he thought; "the same look, the same smile, and about the same age. I wonder if Laura would notice it. I wish she could see him." For a moment he forgot where he was; a far-off memory of his childhood mingled with a recent sorrow. A boy in bare legs wading for pond-lilies, a boy standing by his side watching each stroke of his brush with loving eyes, and the boy before him all seemed one and the same. A strong emotion swept everything from his mind, and he could only stand silent with his eyes fixed on Philip's eloquent face. At length he started like one in a dream, and when he spoke his voice had a new note of tenderness in it.

"What a good boy you are! She's a fortunate little girl to have such a friend. Tell me your name, please; I wish to get better acquainted with you."

The boy flushed with pleasure, and replied promptly, "My name is Philip, M'sieur."

"Philip!" echoed the artist, "how strange! What is your other name?"

"Oh, I'm always called Toinette's Philip. I never thought of any other name. I'll ask my mammy to-night if I've got another."

"Is Toinette your mother?"

"No, M'sieur, she's my mammy. She's a yellow woman, and you see I'm white."

"Have you always lived with Toinette?"

"Always, ever since I can remember."

"Then you have no parents?"

"Parents? Oh, no, I guess not. I don't know; I'll ask Mammy."

"Where do you live?"

"I live on Ursulines street, away down-town. Mammy has a garden and sells flowers. It's a right pretty garden. Won't you come some day to see it? Mammy's proud of her garden, and likes strangers to see it."

"Thank you, certainly I will come," replied the artist, promptly. "I like flowers myself, and I like pictures. I wonder if you like them—I mean pictures. I suppose you have not seen many."

"Lots of them, and I like them too. I've seen them in the churches, and in the shop-windows, and—I've tried to make some," added Philip, lowering his voice and flushing a little.

"Well, my boy, I'm a painter. I paint pictures. Would you like to come and see mine?"

"Yes, M'sieur, I would if Mammy says I may. I'll ask her, and if she'll let me, I'll come to-morrow."

"I wish you could bring your little friend with you. I should like to paint a picture of her," and the artist turned his eyes on the anxious face of the little girl, who was looking eagerly at the note fluttering in his hand.

"Will you go with me, Dea?" asked Philip.

"I can't—I must sell Esmeralda," returned the child, curtly.

The artist looked smilingly from one to the other. "So you have a figure of Esmeralda, and your name is Dea. Where is Homo, the wolf?"

"Homo's under the table, asleep; but he's not a wolf, he's only a wolf-dog."

At this moment, hearing his name used so freely, Homo came slowly out and sniffed at the stranger, who patted his head kindly. Then the old dog with a wag of approbation returned to his nap beside Lilybel.

"Really," thought the artist, with a puzzled look, "it is very interesting. This child and the dog seem to have stepped out of one of Victor Hugo's books."

Here Seline made an expressive pantomime behind Dea, which led the artist to suspect that the modeler in wax was an enthusiast on the subject of the great French writer, and without further explanation, he understood the situation pretty correctly. A poor sick genius—sick mentally and physically, with this one child, who was his only companion and friend.

After a moment of deliberation he said gently, "My child, if you will come to my studio, I will pay you for your time, and I will buy some more of your little figures. I won't keep you long, and it will be better than staying in the street all day."

"Yes, honey, so it will," interposed Seline. "Does yer un'stand? M'sieur'll pay yer, an' yer'll have plenty money fer yer *pauv'* papa."

Dea hesitated, and then replied doubtfully, "I'm afraid papa won't be willing. I'll ask him, but I must go home now. I must—I must go to papa."

"Dea can't promise now," said Philip excusingly; "but perhaps she'll come to-morrow. I'll try to bring her, M'sieur."

"Thank you. I live in that tall house just below here. Ask the cobbler in the court to show you the way to Mr. Ainsworth's apartment," and as the artist gave Philip these directions, he handed the five-dollar note to Dea, who took it with an eloquent glance of gratitude.

"Oh, M'sieur, I'm so glad! Yes, I'll try to come; when *pauv'* papa knows how good you are, perhaps he'll let me come. And may I bring Esmeralda? Will you buy Esmeralda?"

"Yes, I'll buy Esmeralda," returned the artist, with a smile. "You'll find me a good customer, if you'll bring your figures to my studio."

"I'll come—I'll come to-morrow!" she cried eagerly. "Now Seline, give me my basket. I must run all the way to papa."

"Don't, honey, don't get so flustered," said Seline, soothingly, as she handed the basket, "an' don't run. It'll make yer little head ache, an' then yer can't get yer papa's dinner."

"I must—I must run, Seline!" cried Dea. "Au revoir, M'sieur. Au revoir, Philip," and with a happy smile, she darted out of the portico, and down Rue Royale, followed by Homo, who seemed aware of his little mistress's good fortune, for he was now as alert and lively as he was listless and discouraged before.

"Oh, M'sieur, you've done a good deed buyin' dat little image." said Seline gratefully, as she looked after Dea. "Pore child, she's so glad she can't wait, 'cause her papa ain't had no breakfast."

"Nor no supper last night," continued Philip. "Dea don't like to tell, but I always know when they have nothing to eat."

"What! Is it possible?—nothing to eat! Are they as poor as that?" exclaimed the artist. "And have they no one to take care of them?"

"They haven't any one," returned Philip. "They came here from France when Dea was a baby, and her father's been strange and sick ever since her mother died."

"An' that pore chile has to take care of him," sighed Seline. "Oh, M'sieur, do buy somethin' more fer the sake of that motherless little cretur!"

"I will—I certainly will. I'll try to do something for them," replied the painter, kindly. "I'll sell some to my friends. Bring the child to me and I'll see what I can do." Then, with a pleasant "good day" he walked off carrying Quasimodo very carefully.

Philip watched him with admiring eyes until his tall figure disappeared in the court of the high house on the next square; then he turned to Seline and said earnestly, "I didn't think any one who painted pictures would stop to talk to us. Why, I ain't a bit afraid of him. You can bet I'm going to see him, and I'm going to get him to teach me to paint pictures."

"An' he's rich!—he'll buy lots of them little images," returned Seline with undisguised satisfaction.

CHAPTER VI

TOINETTE

MANY years ago when handsome residences were not numerous in the French quarter of New Orleans, the creoles of Ursulines street were very proud of the Detrava place. It was a large white mansion, with fluted columns and wide shady galleries, set well back from the street, and surrounded by a broad lawn and lovely rose-garden, which were hidden from inquisitive neighbors by a high brick wall covered with pink stucco. On each side of the wide gate of beautifully wrought iron were massive pillars, supporting couchant lions, who held beneath their iron paws two rusty cannon-balls brought from the victorious field of Chalmette by the General Detrava who built the imposing mansion, and retired there after the battle of New Orleans.

For many years the Detrava place was the scene of the most generous hospitality, and many an aged lady can count her début at a Detrava ball as one of the most brilliant events of her life. Children and grandchildren succeeded the General, until at last one by one they dropped away, and all were gone but Charles Detrava, a wealthy sugar-planter, who preferred to live in the country on his fine plantation. For years the old mansion was closed and deserted; but at last one winter it was thrown open for a brilliant occasion—the début of the only child, the charming Estelle Detrava, who had just been graduated at the Dominican convent. And that fête will always be remembered by those who were fortunate enough to be present. It was the winter before the beginning of the civil war, and it was almost the last brilliant social event that preceded years of sorrow and disaster.

Among the first to join the Confederate army was Charles Detrava. He went away with his regiment, never to return, leaving his wife and daughter in the seclusion of their country home. Shortly after her husband's departure, Mrs. Detrava died, and Estelle was left without a relative, excepting some cousins in France, whom she had never seen. Then there came a rumor of her marriage, but to whom she was married no one seemed to know; and so little was she thought of in the face of graver events that, some time after, when one night the residents of Unsulines street were awakened by the uproar of a great conflagration, and the old Detrava mansion disappeared in smoke and flames, they were appalled and astonished to learn that a young mother, with her babe and nurse, had perished in the fire. No one knew that the house had been occupied, or that Estelle Detrava, who had lost her husband in a recent skirmish near her country home, had fled from the scene of the conflict to the refuge of the deserted city mansion. She had arrived the day before with her child and servant, and only one or two tradespeople were aware of her being there until the sad news was reported that of the three sleeping in the house that night not one escaped.

TOINETTE AND PHILIP BEFORE THE OLD DETRAVA GATE.

By this sudden and terrible calamity, the family was, as it were, destroyed, as well as the beautiful old mansion, of which there only remained some broken columns and tottering chimneys standing among piles of debris; but very soon that artist, Nature, decorated and beautified the ruins by covering them with a luxuriant growth of flowers and vines, and the curious who stopped to peer through the iron gates, saw only a profusion of green covering the fluted columns and the winding shell-walks.

In the spring the Pittosporum-trees, which before had been kept carefully trimmed, thrust their white blossoming branches above the walls, and the riotous vines climbed over the gate, and almost hid the white board on which was printed in black letters, "*À vendre ou à louer.*" Day after day the sign hung there, in sun and rain, but no tenant came to occupy the little cottage in the rear which had escaped the conflagration, neither did a purchaser appear to bargain for the property that had passed to the next of kin—the unknown cousins in France.

Time passed on, and each season the place looked more neglected and deserted. The beautiful lawn and rose-garden were over-run with weeds, the flowering shrubs grew into trees, the climbing roses and jasmines pushed their branches upward and clung to every possible support, dense shadows brooded among the foliage, where numerous birds built their nests and bred their young. The old garden was still lovely, but a cloud hung over it: the memory of the tragedy of that terrible night. And after awhile foolish rumors filled the neighborhood, and people began to eye the rusty gate and grim lions as though they inclosed and guarded a gloomy secret, until it seemed as if no one could be found who would brave the loneliness and seclusion of the place and take possession of the comfortable little cottage that had served as servants' quarters in the prosperous days of the old mansion.

At last one day the neighbors noticed a respectable-looking old quadroon, leading a lovely little white child by the hand, pass slowly up the street and stop before the gate of the Detrava place. She was a small, gentle-looking woman, dressed in rusty black, with a white *tignon* tied neatly over her gray hair, and the child, though plainly clad, was as clean and fresh as a lily. For a long time the woman lingered with her face pressed against the iron scrollwork of the gate, and when, after some time, she walked sadly away, there were traces of tears on her cheeks.

A few mornings after that, the druggist opposite noticed a slender column of smoke rising from the chimney of the little cottage, and he knew that at last the Detrava place had found an occupant. The old sign disappeared, and after awhile in its place hung another, on which was neatly painted, "Floral designs for funerals and weddings, and cut flowers for sale at very low prices."

It was some time before the curiosity of the neighbors was gratified in regard to the new tenant; and when at last they learned that it was the little quadroon woman who had been seen looking in the gate, they were greatly surprised and disappointed. In spite of every effort, the most they could learn was that her name was Toinette, that she was a skilful florist, and that she was nurse and guardian to the little white boy she called Philip. She was very seldom seen, as she passed in and out of the gate in the rear, and of the child they had only occasional glimpses, and those were at times when he ran, like some lovely little sylvan creature, down the shaded walk between the great oaks and magnolias, to press his round pink face against the iron gate, where he would stand and look out into the narrow, dusty street, his blue eyes wide and bright with pleased surprise. The little creoles on the other side of the gate tried by every means in their power to overcome his shyness, but in vain; at the first approach he would scurry away, and conceal himself behind a clump of bushes or a tangle of vines, until his would-be friends had departed.

He was a healthy, happy child; he loved flowers and birds; all dumb things came to him with the utmost confidence. He was always surrounded by his pets, and they seemed to have a sort of secret understanding with him. Toinette sometimes thought they even had a language in common; for when he whistled softly, the cardinals and mocking-birds flew down to eat out of his hand. He would flit about among the flowers, and butterflies and other winged insects hovered over him. Very early he showed a taste for drawing birds and animals, and Toinette encouraged it. She bought him paper and a small box of colors, and when Père Josef, the kind little priest who lived in a tiny cottage near, told Toinette that the child had talent and would make a painter some day, she was delighted. As soon as he was old enough to learn his letters, she engaged Père Josef to teach him, and every morning, summer and winter, at six o'clock the rosy little fellow finished his hominy and milk, and ran to Père Josef, who was always sitting over his coffee and books at that hour. Philip loved Père Josef, but he adored Toinette. There was nothing in her power that she would not undertake for the child, and he repaid her with ready obedience and unstinted affection; and, as he grew older, he assisted her in many ways: he weeded her flower-beds, transplanted her violets, gathered up dead leaves, and dug the grass out of the cracks of the brick paving with the most patient industry. Therefore, when one day Toinette told him he could go on the street and sell a few flowers, he was overjoyed. He was about six years old then, and he had lost much of the shyness of his infancy; but about him there was always something of the air of a little woodland creature, which made him so natural and charming, and this perhaps led him to seek the protection of Seline when he found himself alone in the crowded streets. He usually sold his flowers in the morning to gentlemen on the way to their offices. He had many regular customers who dropped the dime into his hand as much for the charm of his sunny smile and pleasant "good morning" as for the love of the flowers. When his tray was empty, he did not linger nor idle away his time, but ran off to Toinette, as happy as a lark, to assist her in cultivating her beds of pansies and violets.

Philip had told his mammy of his acquaintance with Dea, and the kind old woman, although she had never seen the little girl, felt a great interest in her, and always managed to supply the boy with food enough for two, so that his little friend need never go hungry. And every day when the boy came home, her question was not whether he had sold his flowers, but whether Dea had sold any of her little figures.

CHAPTER VII

PHILIP ASKS A QUESTION

ON the day when the artist bought Quasimodo, Philip could hardly wait, so eager was he to tell Toinette of Dea's good fortune. So, when his flowers were all sold, he fairly flew down Ursulines street, never stopping for any of the tempting invitations to join in the numerous games the children were playing on the sidewalk; for Toinette's Philip was a great favorite among them, and they were always glad when he appeared.

At the corner of Tremé street he saw a group of boys around a small crippled negro who carried a heavy bucket on his head. "There are the brick-dust children going home, and those boys are tormenting little Bill again!" he cried, with a flash of anger in his blue eyes. "Just let me catch up with them, and I'll scatter them!" A moment after he was in the midst of the crowd, striking out to the right and left. "Look here, you boys; leave that lame child alone! Aren't you ashamed to torment him? Here, Bill, give me your bucket; you can carry my tray," and swinging the heavy pail of brick-dust upon his head, he marched off, as straight as a caryatid, followed by the brick-dust children, who gave three cheers for Toinette's Philip.

When Philip reached the gate of the Detrava place, he was rosy and breathless from his exertion, and his eyes were sparkling with excitement. Toinette was sitting on the little gallery beside a table covered with white flowers. She was filling the wire design of a lamb with small waxen jasmine blossoms.

"Who's that for, Mammy?" asked Philip, leaning against the post of the gallery, while he wiped his hot face.

"It's for a little baby on Prieur street; it died last evening. But what makes you so warm, child?" asked Toinette gently; "haven't I told you not to run so much?"

"I couldn't help it; I was in such a hurry to get home. I wanted to tell you that Dea has sold Quasimodo." Then Philip, rapidly and breathlessly, partly in English, and partly in French, told Toinette of the adventures of the day. "And oh, Mammy, he paints pictures right there where he lives, and he wants me to come to see him! May I go to-morrow?"

"Why, yes, child," replied Toinette, without looking up from her work; "you can go, and if he'll teach you anything, I shall be glad to have you learn."

"He will teach me; I know he will. He's very kind, and he promised to buy Esmeralda," said Philip confidently.

"I'm glad for the poor child," continued Toinette, busily building up the lamb's ears.

"Can't I have my supper now, Mammy? I'm awful hungry. Did you make the gumbo?"

"TOINETTE WAS FILLING THE WIRE DESIGN OF A LAMB WITH JASMINE BLOSSOMS."

"Yes, *cher;* it's all ready. Just wait a minute; I must finish this. The woman's coming for it. I've only got the eyes to put in." And as Toinette spoke she selected the dark leaf of a pansy, and dexterously inserted it into the empty socket. "There, isn't it natural?" she said, holding it off and looking at it admiringly. "It's so white and innocent."

"I don't know," said Philip, regarding it critically, with his head on one side; "I think I'd like the flowers best just as they grew."

At that moment the bell rang, and Philip ran to open the gate. The servant had come with a basket for the lamb.

"Madam will like this," she said as she wiped a tear from her glossy black face; "she doesn't know about it. M'sieur ordered it."

Toinette enveloped the lamb in white oiled paper, and laid it carefully in the basket. She did everything daintily, with a gentle, refined touch; but she looked old and feeble.

"Now, child," she said as the woman went away, walking slowly and glancing often at the basket as if it contained a living thing; "just run and fasten the gate, and I'll set the table for your supper."

Toinette brushed from the little table the fragrant remnants of the flowers, and spread a white cloth over it. Then she went into the spotless kitchen, which served for all their simple needs, and brought out a bowl of steaming gumbo, a dish piled with snowy rice, a plate of biscuit, and a glass pitcher of milk. While she was making these preparations, Philip went to his little bedroom, which opened out of this one living-room, and as he passed through the kitchen, he glanced at everything with a loving eye—how clean and cheerful it looked! The walls were nearly covered with bright wire designs for making floral ornaments for funerals and weddings. These emblems of the extremes of joy and sorrow jostled one another intimately. There were bells and harps, crowns and stars, pillows and horseshoes, gates ajar and four-leaved clovers, lambs and doves, and between these skeleton emblems hung numerous wreaths of white "immortals," on which where mottos in purple, *À mon fils, À ma mère, Priez pour nous,* and the like. The creoles often bought those; therefore Toinette kept them ready with the French mottos. As Philip passed through the room, the evening sun darted in at the west window, and all the frames sparkled like silver. They gave a kind of richness to the place, and set off the white walls, the red brick floor, and the plain dark furniture; outside everything was green and cool, and this bit of light and color made a pleasant contrast. Philip always liked it. Unconsciously his artistic sense was gratified; and, beside, it was his home,—the only one he had ever known,—and it was very dear to him.

He entered his little room and glanced at his white cot, draped with the mosquito-bar, at the little table by the rose-covered window, on which lay his slate and books, and thought proudly in his little heart that there could be no prettier place in the world. A small brown bird hung on a branch of the rose-bush and twittered "Sweety, sweety, sweet!" Philip repeated the caressing notes in a tone exactly like its own, while he bathed his hands and face and brushed his tangled hair; then he took a prayer-book from a shelf over his bed, and went out to the gallery where Toinette was waiting for him. After their simple meal was over, Toinette pushed back her chair and composed herself into a listening attitude.

"Oh, Mammy!" said Philip, coaxingly. as he took the prayer-book and turned the pages; "I'm awful tired—can't I skip the Ten Commandments to-night?"

"Certainly not!" replied Toinette, severely. "Have you ever missed saying them a night since you knew them? Go on, *cher*, I've some work to do before dark, and you have your lessons to learn. Was Père Josef satisfied with you this morning?"

"He said he was. He said I did my *analyse* very well. So you won't let me off to-night? Well, then, I may as well say them."

And Philip, composing his face to a becoming gravity, repeated in a gentle droning voice the Ten Commandments, the Creed, and the Lord's Prayer. When he had finished, Toinette bowed her head and said softly, "Amen." After that serious duty was over he got his books and sat on the steps to study, while Toinette cleared the table and busied herself for some time within. When she came out again she looked at Philip anxiously. The boy was sitting with his chin in his palms and his books were lying neglected at his feet. She glanced again at him; he was in deep thought. What could the child be thinking of? Suddenly Toinette looked older and feebler, and her hands shook as she tried to sort some seeds.

There was something she had been dreading lately. It was a question, and he might ask it at any moment. As he sat there in the soft evening light he looked older to her than he ever had before, and, with an inward shiver, she felt that it was coming.

Suddenly he raised his eyes, and, fixing them on her gravely, he said: "Mammy, that gentleman asked me to-day if my father and mother are living. Are they?"

Toinette turned very pale, and looked away from the child's clear gaze. "No," she replied tremulously; "no, my child, you lost them both when you were a few months old."

"Well, he asked me what my other name was. Have I got another name?"

"Certainly you have," gasped Toinette; "but what need of asking such questions? It can't matter to a little boy like you."

"Yes, Mammy, it does; now I think of it, all boys have two names. Even little Bill is named Bill Brown, and I'm only Toinette's Philip."

A look of pain passed over Toinette's face, and for a moment she remained silent; then she said gravely and decidedly: "You must never ask me any more such questions, Philip. When the right time comes you will know all about it. Some day when I'm not here, Père Josef will tell you. He has some papers for you when you are older; I can't tell you anything now. Forget all about it and attend to your lessons, or Père Josef won't be satisfied with you to-morrow."

Philip picked up his book and fixed his eyes on the page before him, but he did not see it. Suddenly a strange curiosity was awakened in his mind—his mammy would not satisfy it, but perhaps Père Josef would. He would ask him about it in the morning.

CHAPTER VIII

AN ARTIST IN WAX

WHEN Dea reached the small cottage on Villeré street, where she had passed most of the years of her sad little life, she pushed open the creaking gate impetuously, and, closely followed by Homo, ran swiftly up the grass-grown brick walk to the door.

"Papa! papa!" she called, placing her lips to the key-hole. "It's me—it's Dea; do let me in, quick!"

After a few moments of impatient waiting the child heard a slow, listless step approaching, and a hand that seemed weak and trembling turned the key and opened the door cautiously. In the aperture appeared a wan, bearded face, with hollow eyes and tangled hair.

"Papa! oh, papa! just see what I've got." cried Dea, darting through the narrow opening. "I've sold Quasimodo, and I've brought you something to eat"

The man looked at her silently, in a dazed, helpless sort of way, pressing his hand to his head, as if he were trying to collect his thoughts and awaken his memory.

The child was breathless and exhausted from her running; but she closed the door, set down her basket, and then hastened to open one of the blinds, for the room was nearly dark. Then drawing a chair up to a large table, which was covered with books and papers, as well as a number of small wax-figures in different stages of progress, she cleared from one corner of it the numerous articles of her father's craft, and spreading out the napkin containing the food that Seline had given her, she turned to her father, and, putting her arm around him, led him to the chair, and gently seated him.

For a moment he looked at the food silently, while the tears rolled slowly down his thin cheeks. "Is it for me?" he whispered, at length.

"Yes, papa, it's for you. It's all for you."

"No, no; you must eat it, Dea. You are hungry."

"I have had my breakfast, papa; this is for you. Eat it, and see how nice it is," urged the child, as she selected a tempting morsel and held it toward him.

"I'm not hungry; I can't eat. I'm too ill to eat."

"Dear, dear papa, do try. I bought it for you, and I have sold Quasimodo. Look, *cher*, look at the money!" She put her arm around his neck and held the note before him. "Isn't it lovely? Just look, five dollars—twenty-five francs! We sha'n't go hungry again. Oh, dearest, sweetest papa, wake up! try to forget your poor head; try to eat, and get well!" and Dea pressed her anxious little face against his hair and caressed him fondly.

For some time he sat staring at the money, his weak frame shaking with a tearless sob. "It is gone," he groaned at last. "I worked day and night on it. It was the best thing I ever did, and this little piece of paper is all I have for it."

"Oh, papa!" cried the child, with a sharp note of sorrow in her soft voice, "don't think of that. You can do another as good. Think of me, be glad for me, get well for me; I love you, I love you! Try to eat, do try!—this is nice bread, and this is the cheese you like," and, as coaxingly and as tenderly as one would treat a sick child, she broke the food morsel by morsel and put it to his lips.

He did not resist, but ate with pitiful docility, and evidently with little relish. When he would take no more, Dea gave the fragments to Homo, who was watching the result with great interest, as though he was wondering in his dog's heart why his master had to be urged to eat. Then she brought a plate, and, putting the remainder of the food on it, she covered it with the napkin and set it away for another meal. After that she went to her small room, and, slipping off her kerchief and scarf, she put on a long apron that entirely covered her frock—the frock had been one of her mother's, and she was very careful of it; then she proceeded to tidy up the small, neglected chambers. She was so little and frail that the broom in her hands looked out of all proportion, yet she handled it with wonderful dexterity. She swept and dusted and arranged everything with the utmost care; then she returned to the room where her father sat, with his hollow eyes still fixed on the note, his face full of pain and disappointment.

"Let me put the money away, papa," Dea said cheerfully; "and to-morrow I will get you everything you want. Now, I will arrange your table and dust your books."

DEA AND HER FATHER.

There were books bound in leather and books bound in cloth; some had paper covers and some had no covers at all; they were large and small, thick and thin, old and new, but, strange to say, every book bore on its title-page the name of Victor Hugo. Some were beautifully illustrated Paris editions, and these illustrations had suggested certain figures and costumes to the artist in wax, while other studies had been designed and colored entirely by himself, and were the very careful and correct work of no common talent. Under glass cases on a side-table were some exquisite groups, and on the wall hung several

35

medallions of a lovely female head in different positions, as well as a number of studies of a child, all of which bore a remarkable resemblance to Dea. It was not difficult to imagine that Dea's mother had served as a model for the others.

While Dea arranged the table and dusted the books, she talked incessantly, in a low, coaxing voice. At first her father paid little attention to her, then gradually his eyes brightened and his face showed an interest, while from time to time he passed his hand over his forehead and eyes as if he would brush away some object that clouded his vision.

It seemed as though Dea, by repeating what she said, at last impressed the subject on his wandering mind, and claimed his attention almost by force, and in spite of himself.

"Do you understand, *cher?*" she said, impressively. "To-morrow the kind monsieur will buy Esmeralda; then we will have fifty francs, and fifty francs will last a long while. We can have a cutlet and salad for dinner, and old Susette can come and work for us again."

"Fifty francs!—are you sure, Dea, that we shall have fifty francs?" he interrupted with some interest. "Then I can buy some colors. My ultramarine is all gone, and I need some rose madder. I have got to color some wax, and I must have some colors."

"You shall, papa. I'll buy you some to-morrow. You can have everything you want," returned Dea, proudly.

"Can I, my child? Do you think I can? Can I have the Hachette edition of 'L'Homme qui Rit'? There are some fine illustrations in it that I should like to copy."

Dea's little face fell, and her soft voice faltered, "I don't know, papa—I'll see—I'll ask at the shop on the Rue Royale. If it isn't too much, I'll try to get it."

"It ought to be had for fifty francs," said the artist, dreamily.

"But, papa dear, we can't spend the money for books when we have no bread."

"Fifty francs, fifty francs," he repeated complainingly, "and I can't have the Hachette edition?"

"Yes, you can some time. We are going to be rich. Listen, papa, while I tell you: the good monsieur who bought Quasimodo is an artist; he paints pictures instead of modeling *en cire,* and he will pay me to go to his house and sit for him, while he paints a picture."

"But you can't go to his house, Dea, you can't!" exclaimed the artist, excitedly.

"He will pay me, papa, and then I can buy the book."

"Oh, well, if you can buy the Hachette—perhaps you may go."

Dea turned away her head and smiled faintly. "*Pauv'* papa," she thought; "he will consent to almost anything for one of Victor Hugo's books"

"But, papa," she continued tentatively, as she took one of his long, thin hands in hers and stroked it fondly, "I wish you'd let the painter come here and see your groups; he might buy one, and they are worth so much more than the little figures. Can't he come here and see them?"

"Here, Dea!—here in this house, where I am buried? A stranger here, and I so ill, so poor? No, no, child, you are thoughtless, you are cruel! I will never open my door to any one but you," and he glanced around restlessly and anxiously, as if he feared that the stranger was about to effect an entrance.

"Well, never mind, *cher*," said the child, soothingly; "he sha'n't come here if it displeases you. I will take them to him. You can pack them carefully and I will take them."

"Yes, you can take them to him, and I will go to work now and finish something."

In nervous haste he arranged his lamp with its thick shade, selected his wax and small tools, and seated himself at the table with a magnifying-glass adjusted over his eye. He was a tall man, and handsome in spite of his illness; his face was intellectual, and his manners refined and gentle, and as he worked swiftly and skilfully Dea leaned over the table and watched him with fond pride.

After awhile, when the room was quite dark, the child arose and closed the blinds softly; then she went into her father's room, which was next to hers, turned down his bed, drew his mosquito-bar, and placed a carafe of fresh water on the little table. "*Pauv'* papa," she thought, as she went about the room in a gentle, womanly way. "I hope he will sleep to-night, and not groan and walk as he did last night. I must try to get the book; he will be so happy if I get him the book."

When she had finished her preparations for his comfort, she went to say "good night" to him, and, as she kissed him, she whispered anxiously: "Don't sit up late, dear papa; try to sleep to-night, won't you?"

"You're a good child, Dea," he said absently, as he tenderly returned her caress. "Go to your bed, and don't worry about me. I must work now, and later—later, perhaps, I will try to get some rest"

Some hours after, when Dea was sleeping the peaceful sleep of childhood, her father entered her room softly, glanced at her tranquil little face, and at Homo stretched before her bed; then, going to his room, he took his hat, with a band of rusty crape around it, and went quietly out into the sweet moonlit night, closing and locking the door behind him.

CHAPTER IX

The "Children" of Père Josef

THE next morning, when Philip, rosy and fresh after a long night's sleep, ran to Père Josef for his lessons, he found the gentle little priest already seated at his books, with his empty coffee-cup before him.

"Mammy thought I'd be late; I didn't want to wake this morning," said Philip, after the usual salutations were exchanged.

"No, my child, you're in good time; the clock is just on the stroke of six," replied Père Josef, closing his book with an air of pre-occupation; "and I'm glad you're punctual, for His Reverence the Archbishop has sent for me to come to him at nine o'clock. I could not sleep this morning, wondering what such a message betokens. I was up long before dawn, and I thought that idle boy would never bring me my coffee."

While Père Josef was speaking, with some signs of irritation in his usually placid voice, Philip's bright eyes were glancing around the plain little room, as if they were looking for something. At length, failing to see the object of his search, he asked eagerly: "Where are they, Père Josef?—where are the 'children' this morning?"

"*Mes enfants!* Oh, they were so troublesome, so really wicked, that I was obliged to put them in prison. Blanche would sweep the dust all over my books, and Boule-de-Neige covered herself with coffee. Instead of taking her lump of sugar properly, would you believe it? she jumped into my saucer to help herself, and came out with her silky white coat quite ruined. Oh, dear, dear, it was because I was *distrait* that they behaved so badly; they thought I was not noticing them!"

"But, Père Josef, where are they? Can't I see them a moment before I begin my lessons?" asked Philip coaxingly.

"They are locked up in my *armoire*, in the dark. When their spirits are too turbulent, darkness is the only thing that subdues them. Perhaps I have to blame myself for their wickedness, and I don't wish to excuse myself for my folly—I don't want any one to follow my example." Here Père Josef leaned toward Philip and whispered mysteriously, "I shouldn't like any one to know it, my child; but I've been teaching them to dance."

"Oh, Père Josef, how funny that must be! Do let me see them dance!"

"I can't—I can't make them dance now," and Père Josef glanced around furtively. "They won't dance without music—and—and I couldn't play the flute in broad day with the windows open."

"Do you play the flute, Père Josef?" asked Philip, his blue eyes full of mirth. "How pretty it must be to see your 'children' dance while you play the flute."

"Yes, it *is* very amusing. I feel young again when I play the flute for them. It was long ago, when I was a boy at the Seminary, that I learned to play, and I was enchanted with it; but when I took orders I had to give it up."

"But why did you *have* to give it up, Père Josef?" asked Philip with gentle sympathy.

"Because, my dear child, when we offer ourselves to *le Bon Dieu* we must resign many things we love. I loved my flute. It came between me and my duties, and I gave it up; for years and years I never saw it. Now I'm an old man, and I take it out again, I confess it with shame," and a flush of contrition passed over Père Josef's pale, narrow face; "my child, I confess it with shame. I love it as well as I ever did, and, strange to say, I am secretly glad because I remember all the old tunes, and I'm playing them to teach my 'children' how to dance. You're a good, discreet boy, and you won't repeat my confidences. While I'm speaking of it, I may as well tell you of my fears, which prevented my sleeping last night. It seems strange, this summons from the Archbishop. Do you think he can have heard of my folly—my levity, and has he sent for me to reprove me?"

"Oh, Père Josef, you're so good," cried Philip warmly, "the Archbishop won't reprove you for a little thing like that."

"I trust not, I hope not; still I am anxious. His Reverence may have heard of it, and he may think that I am not attending to my duties; but, my dear boy, I have been very careful not to allow my 'children' to interfere with my work, and I have never played on my flute except late at night, or very early in the morning, when others are sleeping."

"If no one heard you," said Philip wisely, "no one could have told His Reverence, so I wouldn't be unhappy about that, Père Josef."

"*Eh bien!* I shall know soon. In the mean time I think my poor 'children' have been punished enough. I will let them out for you to have a little glimpse of them before you begin your lessons. They are charming this morning."

As he spoke, Père Josef went briskly into his little sleeping-room, and presently returned, bringing a small wire cage in which were a number of tiny white mice. As he set the cage on the table the lively little animals began to scamper and scurry from one side to the other of their small house, their little upright ears and pink eyes looking very alert and mischievous.

"Oh, look, look!" cried Philip, "they are playing *Colin-Maillard.*"

"The little rogues, their punishment hasn't done them the least good," said Père Josef, standing off and looking at them admiringly.

"PÈRE JOSEF SOFTLY WHISTLED AN OLD WALTZ."

Suddenly one of the tiniest seized a small broom, made by cutting short the handle of a brush for water-colors, and began sweeping the floor of the cage furiously, making a great fuss and confusion, as she scattered her companions to the right and left. When she had finished this domestic duty to her

41

satisfaction, she shouldered her broom and trotted off on her hind legs to stand it carefully in one corner.

"Is n't Blanche amusing this morning?" said Philip, as he hung enraptured over the cage; "and look at poor Boule-de-Neige with her little coat all coffee-stained; how unhappy she seems! Now, Père Josef, can't you drill them for just a minute? I haven't seen them drill for ever so long."

Père Josef could not resist the temptation to show off the accomplishments of his 'children,' so he seated himself, and, with his thin dark face close to Philip's rosy cheeks as they pressed near the cage, began in a clear distinct voice an exercise which they followed exactly, marching in single file, closing up, and facing to the right or left as they were ordered, standing erect on their little hind legs and going through their manœuvers with the greatest gravity and precision.

Philip was almost beside himself with delight; they were wonderful, they were enchanting! and while he and Père Josef watched their antics they paid no heed to the flight of time. After they had finished their miniature drill, Père Josef softly, and with several nervous glances in the direction of doors and windows, whistled an old waltz, and straightway the tiny sprites began to step and whirl in time to the tune; and never did Pan in a sylvan dell pipe to merrier little elves than these; and while Pan piped and the elves danced Philip's books lay neglected, and Père Josef had forgotten the summons of His Reverence the Archbishop.

Suddenly the little priest started up and looked at his clock in dismay; he had spent nearly an hour amusing himself with his 'children.' Taking a red-and-yellow silk handkerchief he threw it resolutely over the cage, and, turning to Philip, he said: "Come, come, my child, we are wasting our time,—and that is wrong. The little rogues are so fascinating that I forget where I am when I watch them. Perhaps, after all, the Archbishop would do no more than his duty if he reproved me for such a foolish infatuation."

Philip took his books rather reluctantly, and, as he tried to study, he seemed to see the tiny white "children" of Père Josef dancing and whirling between the letters.

When the clock struck eight he was obliged to leave, so he picked up his books hurriedly, and went away without ever thinking of the question he had intended to ask Père Josef.

CHAPTER X

THE LITTLE MODELS

MR. AINSWORTH was sitting at his easel in his improvised studio on an upper floor of the high house on Rue Royale. Although it was only a temporary arrangement, the room was really lovely. On the walls, which were artistically draped with rich foreign stuffs, were a great many charming sketches. About the room, on tables, on brackets, and even on the floor, were bright-colored jars and pots filled with palms, ferns, and various slender-leaved graceful plants, which gave the place a cool, bowery effect. There were pictures on the easels, old china and bronzes on the shelves, books and magazines scattered about in the negligent fashion affected by artists. On a low sofa, covered with a Turkish rug, lay a young woman; she was slender and dark, and her thin cheeks had a feverish flush. One hand was under her head, the other held a book, at which she did not even glance. She wore a loose white woolen gown heavily embroidered with black, and a rich black shawl was folded over her feet. She would have been handsome had she not looked so ill and unhappy. From time to time she coughed and moved restlessly. The sofa was drawn up to an open window, through which the soft spring air entered, gently rustling the slender spikes of the palm that shaded it.

Mr. Ainsworth was putting the finishing-touches to a pretty bayou scene; he was working very busily; at length he looked up and said anxiously: "Is n't there too much wind from that window, Laura?"

"No," she returned in a weak, fretful voice. "I can't live without air. As it is I can scarcely breathe."

"Are you feeling worse this morning, dear?" questioned Mr. Ainsworth gently, still touching his picture carefully and deftly.

"I don't know, really. I feel so badly all the time. It seems as if my weakness increased."

"My darling, you are fretting yourself to death. Try to get above your sorrow. Try, as I do. I try to forget; I try to work."

"I can't forget, Edward; I don't want to forget. It is six months to-day since we lost him—our boy, our only one. Oh, what have we done to be so afflicted!" she cried bitterly.

"Dear Laura, don't look at it in that way. It may not have been to punish us; it may have been infinite love for our child. Try to think so, dear, and it will lighten your sorrow. Cheer up for my sake. You have this heavenly spring morning. Listen to the birds singing in the court below; smell the perfume of the orange-blossoms, the jasmine, the roses; look at the sunlight on the roofs, see how the golden rays burnish that royal magnolia in the garden opposite."

"There are no singing birds, no perfumes, no sunlight for him in his dark little grave," she cried, with a passionate outburst of tears.

"Try to look away from his grave; think of life instead of death; think of other children who live and only live to suffer; think of the sad life of that child I bought the wax figure from yesterday," and Mr. Ainsworth glanced at Quasimodo, standing in state on a bracket with a piece of royal purple velvet behind him. "The little girl interested me, Laura, but not so much as did the boy. Don't think I'm fanciful, but it seems to me that he looks remarkably like our boy. He is about the same age, and, strange to say, *his* name is Philip."

"The same name; that is a singular coincidence," said Mrs. Ainsworth, rising languidly and looking slightly interested; "but I don't see how a little street-gamin can resemble our boy."

"My dear, he doesn't seem a street-gamin. He seems singularly gentle and refined; but you will see for yourself. I think they will come this morning. The poor little girl is so anxious to sell Esmeralda, and the boy was so interested when I told him about my pictures. You should have seen his blue eyes light up."

"Has he *blue* eyes?"

"Yes, that deep violet blue like our boy's, and the same thick curling brown hair. Of course his clothes were plain, but they were clean, and he looked so fresh and sweet—a child that any one could love."

Even while Mr. Ainsworth was speaking there was a timid knock at the door, and when he answered it, there stood the two charming little models, shy and tremulous, but with a determined expression on each small face.

"You see, I've brought Dea," said Philip, sweetly elated at his success. He looked very handsome; he was warm and rosy, and the heavy curls lay in damp rings on his white forehead. Toinette had dressed him in his best suit, a white linen shirt and new blue trousers; he held in one hand a straw hat and with the other he clasped Dea, as if he feared she might escape even then.

The little girl's softly tinted face was very expressive, her eyes were full of expectation and surprise, her lips were parted in a faint, shy smile. She looked healthier and happier and altogether very lovely; with one hand she clung to Philip, and with the other she carried the small basket in which Esmeralda's fanciful costume and the gilded horns of the goat made a bright bit of color.

Mr. Ainsworth's face beamed with satisfaction as he led the children to his wife. "Here, Laura," he said smilingly, "here are my little models. What do you think of them?"

Mrs. Ainsworth did not notice Dea, but her dark eyes rested on Philip with a strange bewilderment of pain and surprise. She did not speak, but after a moment of silence she turned away her head, and covering her face with her thin hands began to cry passionately.

"She sees the likeness as I did," thought Mr. Ainsworth, as he led the children to another part of the room; he did not wish them to be distressed by the sight of his wife's sorrow. With great tact he first sought to amuse and interest them by friendly little attentions. He showed them his curios, his pictures, his flowers; he gave them fruit and bonbons; he slipped a five-dollar note into Dea's basket, and installed Esmeralda on the bracket beside Quasimodo; and after awhile, when they were quite at home, he put a fresh canvas on his easel and posed them for a study. Philip was a little restless, at first; he wished to see the actual picture making, and would have preferred to watch Mr. Ainsworth at his work. But Dea stood like a small statue; she was accustomed to it; she had patiently sat many an hour for her father.

While Mr. Ainsworth painted, completely absorbed in his fascinating little subjects, Mrs. Ainsworth drew an easy-chair near the children and sat silently looking at Philip. Mr. Ainsworth wished to make their first visit so agreeable that they would like to come again; therefore while he worked he chatted pleasantly to them and encouraged them to talk freely to him in return. He was interested to know by what means the artist in wax had been brought to consent to his proposal. After several discreet questions he drew from Dea the shy avowal, that she had come to earn the money to buy the Hachette edition, and that her *pauv'* papa had allowed her to sit for the painter in the hope that she would get him the much-coveted book.

While Dea told her touching little story, Mr. Ainsworth glanced at his wife; she was looking at Philip, but she was listening to Dea. There was a softer expression on her face, and she looked less unhappy.

At last, after a fairly long sitting, the artist told his little models that he was done with them for the morning, and they were as pleased to regain their liberty as a pair of birds would be that had been unexpectedly caged for an hour.

"We must go now," said Philip, with lingering and longing looks at the canvas, on which there already appeared a fair study of himself and his little companion. "I'd like to stay and watch you paint, but I can't to-day. Seline is taking care of my flowers, and I must go and sell them."

"And Homo is asleep under her table," joined in Dea; "I told him to wait for me, and he'll think I'm not coming."

"But you will be sure to be here to-morrow?" said Mr. Ainsworth, looking from one to the other. "Here is your pay for being such good little models," and as he spoke he handed a bright silver dollar to each.

Philip smiled delightedly. "Thank you, monsieur," he said; "I would have to sell flowers all day to make as much."

Dea's little face was a study; she turned the dollar over and over and looked at it as though she doubted her senses. "A dollar—five francs!" she said joyfully. "Oh, monsieur, is it enough to buy the book?"

"No, my dear, I think not; but when you come to-morrow I will see what can be done."

"And, monsieur, may I—may I bring one of papa's groups for you to look at?" asked Dea, hesitatingly. "There's one of the 'Toilers.' It is very pretty."

"The 'Toilers'?"

"Yes, monsieur, 'The Toilers of the Sea.' May I bring it?"

"Why, certainly, my dear. I should like to see it. If I don't buy it myself, some of my friends may."

"But, monsieur, it is very dear; papa says it is worth a hundred francs. It is large, you know—as large as this," and Dea held her small hands apart to give the artist some idea of the size.

"It's too large for you to bring, isn't it?"

"Philip will help me," she said confidently.

"Yes, I'll help you, Dea. It's too big for a girl like you, but it's not too big for me. Come on, now, let's go." Then, turning politely, he held out his hand to Mrs. Ainsworth. "Good-by," he said sweetly.

Mrs. Ainsworth took the little brown hand and drew the boy close to her; for a moment she looked into his eyes, then she put her arms around him and kissed him. Dea came forward and also received a kind caress. It was kind, but it was not like the kiss she had given Philip.

"They are charming," she said, looking at her husband with a smile, the first he had seen on her lips for many a day.

"*Au revoir*, monsieur," said Dea at the door. Philip was halfway downstairs in his impatience to show his bright dollar to Seline.

"*Au revoir*. I will bring the 'Toilers' to-morrow."

CHAPTER XI

PÈRE JOSEF'S SACRIFICE

WHEN Philip and Dea ran to Seline and showed her the bright dollars they had earned so quickly, the good woman was delighted. "Now, chil'run, you's on der way to git rich," she said, showing her white teeth in a generous smile. "I wish m'sieur would wan'ter paint my Lilybel; but he's too ugly. Lilybel's er fright, he is, an' I don't see how cum dat boy's so plain; his pa was a right hansum man, and his two little sisters was as pretty chil'run as you ever seed. Sometimes, when I gets ter studyin' 'bout Lilybel, I's most outdone," and Seline's broad smile changed to an expression of great perplexity. "I ain't jes' sure ef dat boy means ter tell lies, er if he 'magines what he done tole; he's got a powerful 'magination, Lilybel has, an' a awful weak mem'ry. Anyhow, I can't put no conference in dat chile; I's done found out 'bout dat story he tole, chil'run; *he ain't never fall in der ruver!* He jus' sot down with er pa'sel of triflin' chil'run an' stuffed heself with dem cakes an' pralines, an' forgot ter bring der basket home."

Philip and Dea expressed their opinion of Lilybel's too vivid imagination in a way that comforted Seline greatly; their happiness was hers, and very soon she forgot her own troubles in listening to their glowing account of the morning's adventures.

"Seline, it's the most beautiful place you ever saw; and he's got lots of pictures! He's painted them himself. He wants us to come again; and Madam kissed us both—didn't she, Dea?—and told us to come to-morrow."

"And I am to bring the 'Toilers,'" exclaimed Dea, her little face tremulous with excitement. "Monsieur is going to help me sell it for a hundred francs; *pauv'* papa will be so happy."

"My, my! a hundred francs! Yer is in luck, chile; yer's goin ter be rich, shore; an', Mars' Philip, I's done sole all yer flowers while yer's been gettin' yer dollar. I s'pose yer wants ter run home ter tell yer mammy all dem good newses; here's yer dimes"; and Seline dropped a handful of silver into Philip's outstretched palm. Then, as happy and blithe as two singing birds, the children hurried to their respective homes to tell of their good fortune.

When Philip opened the gate and saw Toinette with folded hands sitting quietly on the little gallery, he was alarmed. It was so unusual to see her idle that he thought she was ill. "What's the matter, Mammy?" he called out anxiously before he reached her.

"Nothing, *cher*," she replied, as she took off his hat and stroked his damp hair. "I had no orders for this evening, and I was tired, so I dropped down here to rest; I can't work so hard as I used to."

"Well, you needn't to, Mammy. I can earn lots for you. Just look at this," and he drew out his bright dollar. "All this for an hour or two!"

"The artist must be very generous," said Toinette. "Did he give Dea as much?"

"Yes, Mammy, he gave Dea the same. I wish you could see the picture of us he's painting; he's got Dea's red frock and my blue trousers just as natural!— when it's done I'm going to take you to see it."

"It's a long way to go, my child, and I may not be able. I'm not so strong as I used to be; but put your money away; keep it for yourself—it's yours."

"No, Mammy, you take it. It's for you; all I earn is for you," said Philip, his eyes filled with love and generosity as he urged it upon her.

"Well, we will lock it up in the box, and when you need it for something, you shall have it. And now, my child, I want you to help me. I must transplant these pansies this evening, and for some reason I felt as if I couldn't begin until you came."

"I'll help you, Mammy dear; just let me take off my best clothes," said Philip, cheerfully, as he ran to his room.

"What a good boy he is!" thought Toinette,—"so gentle and obedient! Dear, dear child, who will love him as I have?" And as she went slowly down the steps to the garden, she brushed away more than one regretful tear.

A half hour later, Philip, in his every-day clothes, was working away busily at the pansies, while Toinette sat on a little stool beside him, directing him how to set them. The boy, with his brown head bent over the new earth, was whistling softly. Presently a beautiful cardinal-bird flew down and began fluttering familiarly about his small spade. "Go away, Major," he said, without stopping; "I can't play with you now, but there's a nice fat worm for you." The bird gave a low trill of thanks, seized the unwilling worm, and flew off to a near bush, where he chirped contentedly to his mate.

"Hello, there's the Singer!" said Philip after a moment. "I knew he'd come." As he spoke a mocking-bird over his head burst into a clear, impatient song, circling rapidly around, and brushing him with his wings as if to attract his attention.

"It's strange," said Toinette, musingly, "how birds and butterflies come around you; they never fear you. I suppose it's because you never hurt them."

"It's because I love them and they know it,—that's why they come. I've lived here a long time with them; it's our home; we're all one family, and, Mammy, you're the dear old mother-bird."

He kept on working with his bright head bent, and he did not see the tears in Toinette's eyes. It was very lovely and peaceful. The place was full of sweet scents and sounds. The broken white columns, covered with a profusion of roses and jasmine, looked like a bower in a sylvan nook of Arcady. The ruins of the Detrava mansion were mounds of green and bloom; there was nothing dreary, nothing unsightly, no suggestion of age and decay; but all spoke of youth—fresh, eternal youth. Perhaps it was the strong contrast of the boy, the flowers, and the singing birds that made Toinette feel so old and feeble as she sat there, her toil-worn hands folded on her lap, and her dim eyes fixed with a tender, protecting love on the merry little fellow who worked in happy unconsciousness of the sorrows of age.

Presently the gate-bell rang, and its loud jangle startled Philip from his work and Toinette from her reverie. "Run, child! it is some one in a hurry"; and Toinette left her seat and hastened to meet the new-comer. It was Père Josef. He walked up the path very hurriedly, brushing the obtrusive roses with the skirts of his worn black coat. His narrow dark face wore an expression of mingled surprise and sorrow. In one hand he carried a bundle tied up in a red-and-yellow handkerchief. Without glancing to the right or left, he hastened up the steps to the gallery, and set the bundle on the small table with an air of resolution.

"Toinette, my good friend! Philip, my dear boy! I've brought them to you. There they are, *mes enfants, mes chers petites enfants.*" He spoke firmly, but in a sad, constrained voice.

Toinette and Philip looked at him, astonished. "Why, Père Josef, why do you do this?" said Toinette.

"Did His Reverence tell you you must?" asked Philip, anxiously. "Did he know about your pets?"

"No, no, my dear boy; he had heard nothing. It was a matter of more importance. I was unwise to think the Archbishop would trouble himself about such folly. He sent for me to give me instructions. I am to leave on a mission. I go to-night."

PÈRE JOSEF'S SACRIFICE.

51

"Oh, Père Josef, to-night! Is it far? Will it be for long?" cried Toinette and Philip in the same breath.

"I can't say. I can't tell you anything. I'm like a ship sailing under sealed orders; but from some remarks of His Reverence, I think it will not be for long. I go to do the work of a brother who is ill. When he recovers, it is likely I shall return."

"But can't you take the 'children' with you, Père Josef?" asked Philip. "You will be so unhappy without them."

"My child, I *might* take them, and I shall be miserable without them; but it would scarcely be proper for a servant of the Church to start on a sacred mission carrying a cage of white mice with him"; and Père Joseph smiled grimly. "It's a sacrifice, a trial; but I must leave them."

"And they have been so much company, such a pleasure to you," said Toinette, with ready sympathy.

"Yes, and that is just where I have done wrong. I have made companions of these innocent little animals,—I have grown to love them,—and now I see that I have neglected my duties. My good friend, I have spent many hours teaching these creatures folly, when I should have been teaching human beings something useful. Life is too short to waste any part of it, but—but they were so innocent, so charming, and really they seemed to love me"; and Père Josef winked and coughed, and rubbed his nose vigorously with his coarse handkerchief.

"I'll be very good to them; I'll take good care of them; and when you come back you'll have them again," said Philip, consolingly.

"I know you'll be kind to them. They're very affectionate, and I don't think they will forget me. When I return, perhaps I will take them again—that is, if I am not too fond of them. However, Philip, I leave them with you; I give them to you until I claim them. Good-by, my dear boy," and he held out his thin hand; "be obedient and studious while I am gone, and don't—don't neglect my 'children.'" And without as much as glancing at the bundle on the table, Père Josef turned away and walked hurriedly down the path, followed closely by Toinette.

So busy was Philip taking the covering off the cage, that he did not notice how earnestly Toinette and the priest were talking as they stopped for a moment near the gate. With his hand on the latch, Père Josef was saying: "The papers will be safe during my absence. I leave them with mine, in the care of a friend. If you need them before I return, he will give them to you"; and he mentioned a name and address.

Toinette replied: "I hope I shall not need them, and that when you come back you will find everything as it is now."

"I trust so, my good Toinette. We are in the hands of God. *Au revoir*—not adieu."

As Philip looked up he saw the black figure of Père Josef vanish through the gate, and again he thought: "I didn't ask Père Josef, after all; and now he is gone. Well, I must wait until he comes back."

CHAPTER XII

A Surprise

"SUSETTE, do you know it is papa's birthday?" said Dea one morning to the old woman who often came to cook and do heavy work for the little housekeeper.

"No, Ma'mselle, I didn't know it, but I'm thankful your papa is here to see another birthday—and so much better than he was. Why, he's like another man!"

"He smiled this morning when I wished him *bon jour*," said Dea, her own serious little face dimpling at the pleasant thought; "and it's the first time for so long. Yes, he's better and happier, and I want him to have a good birthday dinner. I want you to go to market. He must have some soup and fish, and a nice little chicken, some peas, and a salad; and I am going to surprise him with some fruit, because, Susette, we are almost rich now, and it is his birthday."

"Very well, Ma'mselle; I will do just what you wish," returned the old woman, with pleased alacrity.

"And, Susette, don't say anything to papa. I want to surprise him. You will cook the dinner nicely, and I will arrange the table. Philip has promised me some flowers, and Seline is going to make me a birthday cake; I will bring them when I come from monsieur's. Now don't disturb papa, because he is very busy; he is working on an order—he is making a medallion of monsieur's little boy, who is dead. He is making it from a photograph, and it is such a pretty face. Papa is so interested in it. When it is finished, I am to take it to monsieur, and he will pay a great deal for it. Now please be very quiet and careful, Susette."

"I will, Ma'mselle, I will," replied the old woman, looking at Dea doatingly; "and I'll do the marketing as cheap as I can; you won't be ashamed of your papa's birthday dinner."

"*Pauv'* papa, it's so long since he had a birthday, I want this to be a happy one. Now I'm going to hurry to Rue Royale; give me my basket, and I will bring the flowers and cake."

Within a few weeks a great change had taken place in the small cottage on Villeré street. To the poor artist in wax a little success meant a great deal. At last he had found some one to appreciate his peculiar talent, and, ill and suffering though he was, his beclouded mind grasped that fact and held to it. It seemed to give him new life and hope. He saw before him the means of support for himself and the patient, tender little creature who clung to him so faithfully in all his trouble. One by one his beautiful groups and figures had disappeared from his dingy room, to find in Mr. Ainsworth's studio admirers and purchasers; and the careful, mature child, with all the burden of life on her slender shoulders, knew how to economize the generous sums she received for them. Therefore, it was no wonder that when Dea, who a few weeks before had lacked a nickel to buy bread, looked at the little pile of bank-notes locked safely in her father's desk, she thought that she was rich, and could well afford a birthday dinner.

They had not always been so poor. Some years before, when the artist in wax first came from France, he had quite a handsome sum of money. He bought the small cottage in Villeré street, and furnished it neatly for his pretty young wife, a gentle, industrious girl, who had been a governess in a rich family, and who eked out their small income by giving piano-lessons to the little creoles in the neighborhood. The artist, always peculiar, with his strange worship for the great French writer, quietly studied and illustrated the books that he adored. Sometimes he worked with his pencil; but oftener with the plastic medium of wax. Now and then he sold some of his small figures, and occasionally he had an order for a portrait medallion; and in this way the quiet years passed, until the young wife was taken away. After that his health failed, and the heavy burden of existence fell upon the frail child, who was bearing it so bravely.

When Dea reached the studio in Rue Royale, she found Philip already there. He was seated at a table beside Mrs. Ainsworth, with a plate of delicious strawberries before him, and Mr. Ainsworth was working very busily on a charming little study he was making of the group.

These visits to the studio were the beginning of a new life to the boy, and every day the charm of it increased. Mrs. Ainsworth had become deeply interested in him, and treated him with the greatest affection, and Mr. Ainsworth encouraged the intimacy, when he saw his wife more cheerful and in better health. Every day he planned to keep the boy with them as much as possible. After making a great many studies of the little models, he had begun teaching Philip the rudiments of drawing. The boy had brought his rude sketches to the artist, who saw in them evidences of talent, and as Toinette was anxious to have him learn, Mr. Ainsworth found it a pleasure to teach the intelligent, docile little fellow.

Often, when the artist and his wife were alone, they seriously discussed the future of the child, and wondered to what destiny he was born. A vague wish was in the heart of each that neither liked to be the first to express. There was one thing of which they were certain—he was necessary to their happiness; the days were brighter when he came, and sadder when he remained away. They were very fond of Dea; but she had not grown into their hearts as Philip had. It was the striking resemblance to their lost boy— the eyes, the hair, a tone in his voice, in his laugh, a way of looking at them— that made them long to keep him always. The weather was very warm, and often they spoke of going; but day after day they lingered, fascinated with this new affection.

When Dea's radiant face appeared at the door, Philip left his strawberries, and ran joyfully to meet her, saying, "Here are the flowers for your papa's birthday. Mammy sent them to you, with lots of good wishes."

Dea thanked him with a tremulous smile, as she took the beautiful roses and laid them carefully in her basket. Her little heart was very full, and she could not say much.

"Here are some strawberries for you, my dear," said Mrs. Ainsworth, making room beside her; "they were so tempting to Philip that he could not wait until you came."

"If you please, Madam, may I take them home and eat them with papa? It is his birthday."

"Certainly, my child, if you would rather," and Mrs. Ainsworth filled a little basket, and placed it beside the flowers.

"Have you a birthday present for your papa, Dea?" asked Mr. Ainsworth, who was watching the child's varying expression of delight. Her care for her father was half pathetic and half amusing.

"No, Monsieur," she replied, a little sadly; "that is, I haven't much beside the flowers and Seline's cake. I wanted to get the book, but—but it was twenty-five francs, and I could not pay so much."

Mr. Ainsworth looked at his wife and smiled. "Well, my dear, don't be unhappy. Your father shall have the book; he shall have it for his birthday. It is a present from you. You have been such a patient little model that I don't feel as though I had half paid you. I give *you* this to make it up," and he handed her the book, neatly covered with paper tied with a narrow ribbon.

Dea took the package silently. Her softly tinted cheeks turned quite pale, and her eyes seemed to distend with surprise and delight. "Oh, oh!" she gasped at length, "how glad *pauv'* papa will be! I can't thank you now, Monsieur, I can't—I can't!" and bursting into sudden tears of gratitude, she took her basket and hurried away without another word.

When she reached home, her father was still bending over his delicate work, quite unmindful of everything, birthdays included. She said nothing to him. She was pale and excited, and her small face wore a look of great importance.

"Susette," she cried eagerly, as she entered the kitchen, "how is the dinner getting on?"

"Finely, Ma'mselle, finely; I got artichokes, the first in the market, and such a fat chicken, and all for so little; and a handful of meat scraps for Homo for lagnappe."

"And, oh, Susette, I have strawberries! Madam gave me strawberries. What *will* papa say when he sees it all? And the book! the book!"

She was so excited that her fluttering little fingers could scarcely arrange the few pieces of china and silver—the remnants of their better fortunes; but at last, when all was ready, and the book—the much-coveted book—was laid by her father's plate, with the fruit and flowers on each side of the table, and Seline's beautiful cake in the center, she could hardly wait for the dinner to be served. She flitted constantly back and forth between the kitchen and the little dining-room, discussing, inspecting, and directing everything until she went to lead her father to the table.

"Papa, do you know that it is your birthday to-day?" she said, joyfully, as she smoothed his hair and arranged his carelessly tied cravat; "and I want you to look very nice, because I have a surprise—a real surprise—for you."

The artist laid down his tools, removed his glass, and arose with dreamy indifference. "My birthday, dear child? No, I had not thought of it. All days are alike to me, now."

"You won't say so, Papa, when you see what I've got for you. This is a lovely day, a happier day than we've had for a long time."

Then she threw open the door impressively, and proudly seated her father at the pretty table. As he glanced from the flowers to the fruit, his face brightened with pleased surprise, and he said cheerfully, in a tone that enchanted Dea, "Why, my darling, you have indeed surprised me! I little expected such a feast." Then his eyes fell on the book, which he seized eagerly, and pulling off the wrapper, began to devour the contents, glancing greedily from the title-page to the illustrations.

"The Hachette edition, Dea; where did you get it? Is it mine—mine to keep?"

"Yes, Papa, it is yours. Monsieur, the artist, gave it to me for keeping so quiet when I sat for him; and I give it to you. It is a birthday present from me."

"You are a good child, Dea," he said, his eyes fixed on one of the illustrations. "This is excellent; this will make a fine group."

"But, Papa dear, look at the other things. Philip's mammy sent you the flowers. Seline made the cake for you, and madam gave me the strawberries. Aren't they all lovely?"

The artist's eyes wandered slowly over the table. "Yes, my dear, they are beautiful, and your friends are very good to us; but the book—the Hachette— it is the best of all."

During the dinner Dea tried by every art to attract her father's attention from his book. He ate slowly of the good things set before him, with his eyes fixed on the fascinating pages. He was happy in his own way, and the child was satisfied, for she said in confidence to Susette, when the feast was over:

"Dear Papa, how happy he was! He enjoyed his birthday dinner so much. He ate every thing I helped him to—strawberries and cake, and everything. And fancy, Susette, he was looking at his book all the time; but the best part of all was the surprise. Oh, Susette, he was *so* surprised!"

CHAPTER XIII

Philip Says "No"

THE next morning after Dea's birthday dinner, Philip sat on the gallery amusing himself with Père Josef's "children." It was quite early, and Toinette, who was within, attending to her household duties, thought the boy was studying. His books and slate lay on the table near the cage, but he was not looking at them; he could not get interested in his lessons with such merry little rogues scurrying to and fro before him.

"I mustn't let them forget what Père Josef taught them," reasoned Philip; "it would be too bad if they couldn't do their drill when he comes home. I must make them practise a little every morning." Therefore he was putting them through their exercises with quite an easy conscience.

The air was sweet and cool; the sun was just peeping over the pittosporums, which were white with blossoms; the dew lay in sparkling drops on the stars of the jasmine, and every little blade of grass was diamond-tipped; the spiders' webs, stretched across the rose-bushes, looked like spun glass as they waved daintily in the soft wind. Philip's bowl of hominy and milk stood beside him; the Major and the Singer had come to share it. He cared no more for his food than he did for his books; he was intensely interested by the indications of a misunderstanding between his pets. The birds seemed jealous of Père Josef's "children," and fluttered and pecked viciously at the cage, whose tiny occupants scurried from side to side in order to get out of the reach of their unfriendly bills. At last, with a funny little show of bravery, the mice drew themselves up in battle array, and presented a bold front to the enemy.

This so amused Philip that he burst into a hearty peal of laughter, which brought Toinette to the gallery, interested in spite of herself. "Oh, Mammy," he cried, "just watch them for a minute! The Major and the Singer are jealous."

"And the 'children' are frightened," said Toinette. "See them flutter and tremble, in spite of their brave appearance." As she spoke, she took a handful of grain from a box and scattered it on the grass for the unfriendly birds. "Go and eat," she said, "and don't make the poor little things unhappy."

The "children" stood up, gravely watching the motions of the birds, who gave a last threatening peck before they disappeared. When they were finally gone the little sprites began to dance merrily; they imagined *they* had routed the enemy and come off victoriously.

"They're very lively," said Philip, looking at them admiringly. "I don't believe they miss Père Josef."

"No, I don't think they do," returned Toinette, a little sadly. "It's the way with almost everything in this world: 'out of sight, out of mind,'" and she sighed as she dropped into her old rocking-chair and leaned her head against the faded cushion. "I often think, my dear, that if I went away you'd forget me just as soon."

"You're not going away, Mammy," replied Philip, cheerfully; "but if you did, I shouldn't forget you; I couldn't if I tried."

Toinette smiled patiently. "You wouldn't mean to, *cher*; but after awhile, before you knew it, your old mammy would be gone out of your mind. Some one else would take her place. I often study about these strangers from the North; they're a great deal to you already. I don't blame you, my child; they're very good to you; the artist teaches you. Sometimes I think they may want to take you away from me. Would you go, Philip?"

There was just a touch of jealousy in the old woman's patient voice, and her thin, dark face was full of anxiety as she waited for the boy's answer.

It came directly, clear and truthful. "No, Mammy, of course I wouldn't; I wouldn't leave you for any one. I'm happy here, with my birds and flowers and Père Josef's 'children.' I couldn't like any other place, and I couldn't love any one as I love you, Mammy."

Toinette's dim eyes brightened with pleasure. "I'm glad to hear you say that, Philip; I've had you a long time, and I've tried to take good care of you, and to teach you to be good. There's plenty of time for you to learn everything. I couldn't let you go away; I couldn't give you up just yet, but I'm old—old, and perhaps—Well, eat your breakfast, child, and try to study awhile before you go to the studio."

When Philip left Toinette with an affectionate *au revoir*, he did not know how soon again his loyalty would be put to the test. Mr. Ainsworth and his wife were talking very seriously when he entered the studio, with a bright face and a cheerful "good morning."

"Come here, my dear," said Mrs. Ainsworth, drawing him gently down beside her, while she encircled him with her arm. "We want to talk to you. We are thinking of going away soon, and we find it hard to leave you, my dear child. Would you like to go with us?"

Philip's cheeks flushed crimson, and his eyes filled with tears. "Oh, I don't want you to go! I don't want to lose you, but I can't go with you."

"Why can't you, my dear boy? We will do everything for you. We will make you very happy, and you can go on with your drawing," said Mr. Ainsworth, persuasively.

"You can travel and see other places. We will spend the summer in the mountains. You can have a pony, and you can go out sketching with Mr. Ainsworth," urged Mrs. Ainsworth.

"I should like to travel; I should like to see the mountains—I never saw any; and I should like a pony," replied Philip, looking up bravely, while he wiped away his tears; "but I can't go. I can't leave mammy,—she's old, and I've got to stay with her and take care of her."

"If your mammy should consent? If she should think it best for your future? If she should be willing?" asked Mrs. Ainsworth.

"But mammy *wouldn't* be willing," replied Philip, with conviction; "and then there's Dea; I've got to take care of her, and I've got to take care of Père Josef's 'children.' I couldn't leave them," he added gravely, as the weight of his responsibilities pressed upon him.

Mr. Ainsworth looked to his wife for some further argument in their favor. They were thrilled with admiration for the loyal little fellow, and yet they were bitterly disappointed.

"But, my dear boy," said Mrs. Ainsworth, after a moment's silence, "if it were not for your mammy, would you go with us? Do you love us well enough to go with us?" Her hungry heart craved some assurance of the boy's love.

"If it wasn't for mammy, yes, I'd go," he replied readily. "I want to learn to paint pictures, and I'd like to see everything, and—and—you're so good to me. I don't want you to go away," and again the blue eyes filled with tears; "but you see I can't—I can't leave mammy."

"I see you can't, my dear," returned Mrs. Ainsworth, soothingly; "you are a good, loyal boy, and we love you all the better for your devotion to your old nurse. There is a great deal to be thought of on both sides, but we must go on loving you, and you must not forget us, and when we come back next winter we want to find you the same dear boy that you are now."

"We are greatly disappointed, Philip," said Mr. Ainsworth, regretfully. "We are sorry to go without you; but we shall watch over your future, and perhaps when we return we can make some arrangement,—perhaps there will not be so many obstacles in the way."

"If mammy and Père Josef should say I could, and that it was best, I might go for a little while, but I can't leave mammy now, and anyway I must be here when Père Josef comes back."

And that was Philip's ultimatum. No further arguments nor inducements could influence him. There was a serious and secret reason why he must wait for Père Josef's return.

CHAPTER XIV

"I've Come to Stay With You"

PHILIP had not been to the studio for two days, and Mrs. Ainsworth was very unhappy over his absence. It was a week or more after the conversation related in the last chapter, and they had finally decided to leave the next day.

"I can't think what has kept the child away," said Mrs. Ainsworth, complainingly. "He knows we are going to-morrow, and he would certainly be here if something serious had not happened."

"I will go to Seline," said Mr. Ainsworth, taking his hat. "If he hasn't been there, I will send her to look him up." And as he spoke he opened the door to go out, and there stood Philip, who was about to enter. At first Mr. Ainsworth did not notice that Lilybel was hanging back in the shadow of the door, and that he carried a bag and a large basket; but he *did* notice that Philip looked very pale, and altogether unlike himself.

As soon as Mrs. Ainsworth heard her husband exclaim, "Why, Philip! I was just going to see what had become of you," she came forward joyfully, but started back surprised when she saw the boy's face. Then she noticed that he was dressed in black and that around his straw hat was a band of rusty crape, and that his eyes, when he raised them, had the wide, frightened look that one sometimes sees in a lost, helpless animal. He seemed much older, for the charming roundness and color of infancy had vanished, and his cheeks were pale and tear-stained; a few days of weeping and fasting had changed him greatly. When he tried to speak, his lips quivered, and the sobs which he struggled to suppress almost choked him. In one hand he carried a bundle tied up in a red-and-yellow silk handkerchief; in the other, one of Toinette's white wreaths, with the purple motto, *À ma Mère.*

When Philip entered the room, Lilybel slipped in behind him, and putting the basket on the floor, he placed the bag beside it. Then he flattened himself against the wall and stood with his toes turned in and his arms hanging awkwardly, while he twisted his mouth into the most lugubrious contortions and rolled his eyes mournfully.

Mrs. Ainsworth saw nothing but Philip. For a moment she looked at him pityingly; then she took him in her arms and drew him close to her. "My poor child, my darling! Tell me what has happened," she said tenderly.

Philip wiped his eyes and swallowed his sobs resolutely. "Mammy is dead," he replied brokenly, "and—and I've come to stay with you."

"Your mammy is dead! Why, how—when did it happen?" exclaimed Mr. and Mrs. Ainsworth in the same breath.

"It was in the night. She went away while I was asleep. She thought *I* might go and leave her, but now *she's* gone first and left me," said Philip, making a great effort to control his grief, and trying to tell his sad little story calmly and clearly. "Mammy always got up early, and when she didn't come to call me, I went to her room, and she was lying in her bed asleep. I tried to wake her and I couldn't, so I ran to the doctor's on the next block; he came back with me, and he said—he said—dear mammy would never wake again. She had just gone away in her sleep, and she never told me she was going—never said good-by or anything. Then I went for Seline. I knew Seline would come, because Père Josef was away. Père Josef was a good friend to mammy; she always went to him when she was in trouble."

"My dear, dear boy! Why didn't you come to us?" asked Mrs. Ainsworth, who was crying in spite of herself. "We would have done everything for you."

"Well, mammy knew Seline. I didn't think; I ran right to her, and she and Lilybel have stayed with me ever since. We had the funeral yesterday, out at St. Roch's—mammy always said she wanted to be buried there. It's awful quiet there. She had money in a box to pay for everything,—I knew all about it; she showed it to me once and told me it was to bury her with,—and we had two carriages. Père Martin from St. Mary's Church went in one, and Dea and I, with Seline and Lilybel, went in the other, and—and I cut roses enough to cover her grave, because dear mammy won't want any more flowers, she won't make any more crowns and harps!" and, overcome by the thought that these were the last offices for the departed, he hid his face on Mrs. Ainsworth's shoulder and cried passionately.

At that moment there came a low growl from the basket, followed by the wail of a cat, and the peeping and fluttering of fowls.

"You jes' stop dat noise in dar!" cried Lilybel, sharply, at the same time giving the basket an energetic kick, which served only to increase the tumult.

Mrs. Ainsworth started up surprised. "What are those?" she asked, looking at Philip's humble belongings.

"SHE TOOK HIM IN HER ARMS AND DREW HIM CLOSE TO HER."

"They're mine," said Philip, wiping away his tears. "Lilybel brought them. The puppy and the kitten and six little chickens are in the basket. Mammy raised the chickens,—the hen stole her nest and mammy found it; she thought so much of them I couldn't leave them. These are Père Josef's 'children,'"—indicating the bundle in the red-and-yellow handkerchief,—"and this," glancing at the wreath, "I want to keep always to remember dear mammy by. I couldn't leave them, so I brought them this morning, and I've got to take them all with me."

Mr. Ainsworth smiled, but there was a lump in his throat that was difficult to swallow. However, he said gently: "Well, my dear boy, we will see presently what we can do with your family of pets; but, first, do I understand that you have made up your mind to go with us—that you have really decided?"

"Yes, sir; I mean to go. You know I said I'd go if it wasn't for leaving mammy, but now she's left me and there's nothing to hinder; I can't live there without her. I haven't any other home, and Père Josef is gone. I will go with you and stay until he comes back; then he'll tell me what I must do. Seline has locked up everything. There's nothing there now to miss me but the Major and the Singer, and I guess they won't forget me. I guess they'll be there when I come back. Now," he added, with a business-like air, and quite as if everything were settled, "if you'll tell me where I can put those things in the basket, Lilybel and I will let them out; and there are my clothes," pointing out the bag; "my best suit is in there, but I sha'n't wear it now, because I'm in deep mourning. Dea put this crape on my hat; she had it when her mama died. Wasn't she good to think of it?"

Mrs. Ainsworth's heart was deeply touched by the confidence and simplicity of the child; she could only clasp him to her and cry over him, while her husband turned away to smile and wipe off a tear at the same time, so closely united in Philip were the ludicrous and the pathetic.

The artist was at a loss to know how to dispose of the contents of the basket without shaking the boy's confidence, or wounding his feelings. It was a matter difficult to decide upon in a moment. However, he gained time by sending Lilybel down to the court with the "happy family" of animals, where the cobbler and his wife took charge of them until some permanent arrangement could be made for their safety and comfort. But Père Josef's "children" had come to stay. He felt that it would be useless to try to persuade Philip to leave them behind, and he knew that the little cage and its tiny occupants would have to travel with them wherever they went.

CHAPTER XV

THEY VISIT ST. ROCH'S

MR. AND MRS. AINSWORTH were again obliged to delay their departure a day or two, in order to make some new arrangements, owing to this sudden addition to their family. In the first place, Philip's wardrobe was not quite suitable for a fashionable resort in the Adirondacks, where they expected to spend the summer; and then, there were the puppy, the kitten, and the chickens to be disposed of, and various other things to be settled.

They loved Philip very dearly, and enjoyed his presence greatly; but now that he was thrown entirely on their care and protection, they were somewhat dismayed at the responsibility.

"He is a dear boy, and I am so happy to have him," said Mrs. Ainsworth; "and yet, now that he is really ours, I feel some misgivings."

"Yes, it's a very serious matter to adopt a strange child, especially one of whose parents we know nothing," returned Mr. Ainsworth, thoughtfully. "I wonder what mother will say. I'm sure she won't approve of it. You know what strong prejudices she has, Laura."

"But if it is a pleasure to us, she surely won't object. We have had sorrow enough, and if this dear boy fills our empty hearts in the least, or comforts us for the loss of our darling, she ought to be thankful. In any case, I can't see that we are obliged to consult your mother," added Mrs. Ainsworth, with some spirit. "We are the ones to decide whether it is best or not."

"Certainly, my dear, it is entirely our affair. It seems best, it really seems best both for us and the child. Poor forlorn little fellow, his confidence in us is touching, and, Laura dear, there are advantages in his having no kin; we don't know who they might have been. They might have made it impossible for us to have him. Seline, who seems to have been somewhat in Toinette's confidence, says the boy is an orphan without doubt, and that no one has ever attempted to claim him. Of course there is a history and a mystery; but now that the old nurse is dead, I don't see any way to find out. If there had been a possibility of having him while she lived, I should have tried to get the secret from her, although Seline says she was very 'close.' As it is, I think that we can feel that he is entirely ours because he belongs to no one else."

"And I am sure he came from good stock, he has so many fine qualities. He is so truthful, so brave, and so generous, and he has such a plastic, gentle nature that we can mold his character as we wish, and make his deportment perfection in a short time," said Mrs. Ainsworth, hopefully.

"He is a genuine child of nature," returned Mr. Ainsworth. "I don't know how an artificial atmosphere will affect him. I don't know how he will develop, away from his simple, natural life, his flowers, his birds, his blue skies and soft winds."

"Let us hope for the best," said Mrs. Ainsworth, encouragingly. "If he does us no further good, he at least has given me a new interest in life, and that is worth something."

"It is worth everything, my dear. It means life and hope to me as well as to you."

The next morning, after Philip had brought himself and his belongings to Rue Royale, Dea went early to the studio; but the boy had already gone out, and Mrs. Ainsworth, who was there alone, was busily engaged, looking over a package of boy's clothing which had just been sent in for her inspection.

Dea stood beside her and watched her with great interest, as she examined garment after garment—such fine glossy jackets and trousers, such dainty shirts and long, soft stockings, and shoes and hats that were marvels of perfection!

"Are these *all* for Philip?" asked Dea, in her soft little voice, her eyes full of surprise and pleasure.

"Yes, my dear; do you think there are too many?" said Mrs. Ainsworth, with a smile.

"There are a great many. I'm glad Philip will have them; he will look so nice. I hope he will have my crape on his new hat. When he sees it he will think of me. I had it for mama; I wouldn't have given it to any one else."

Philip had gone out very early, and Mrs. Ainsworth told Dea that he had asked to go to St. Roch's to plant some flowers from the Detrava place on Toinette's grave.

"Well, I will go there and help him. I often go there; my mama is buried there, and Toinette's grave is very near hers. It is so peaceful there; there are no sounds—only the leaves rustling, and the birds that sing softly, as if they were afraid of waking those who sleep there. I will go right away and help Philip plant the flowers"; and with a gentle "*Au revoir,*" she slipped out as quietly as she had entered.

When Dea reached the pretty little cemetery, she stood still for a moment at the gate, and looked sadly and thoughtfully toward the shady corner where Philip was busily planting the flowers, and carefully pressing the fresh earth around them. They were Toinette's favorites—violets, pansies, and the slender amaryllis. He had placed a sweet-olive at the head and a jasmine at the foot. "They will bloom first in the spring," he thought, "and she loved them so."

PHILIP AND DEA AT TOINETTE'S GRAVE.

Near was another carefully tended grave. It was covered with lilies and hedged around with fragrant white roses. At the head of the mound, under a glass shade, was an exquisite figure in white wax. It represented the angel of sorrow. The beautiful head was bowed, and the white lips seemed to murmur a prayer. Dea thought this the most beautiful memorial that ever was placed over a sleeping saint.

The face resembled hers, and, as she stood above it with clasped hands, she too seemed like an angel of sorrow. When Philip looked up suddenly and saw her standing there, among the tangle of roses, slim and pale, with soft, downcast eyes, the thought of what he had lost and what he was about to lose filled his heart with sharp pain, and for a moment he gave way to his grief in a passionate flood of tears, kneeling in the long grass and covering his face with his earth-stained hands.

In a moment Dea was kneeling beside him, trying to comfort him with gentle words of sympathy and love. "Don't, Philip, don't cry so; it would hurt your mammy if she knew it. You see I don't cry over mama's grave. Dear mama! she sleeps so sweetly there, and papa's beautiful angel always watches over her day and night."

"Oh, Dea, I'm going away; I'm going so far, and there won't be any one to take care of mammy's grave."

"Yes, Philip, there will; I will take care of it, and at All Saints' I will have the flowers dug and the grass cut. Seline will help me; we will do it together, and when you come back it will be lovely here"

"Oh, Dea! I don't want to go; I can't go," cried Philip, with sudden regret.

"Yes, you must go, Philip; it will be best. Seline says so, and monsieur says so; but you must come back when Père Josef returns. Now, you have planted all your flowers, come into the chapel and say a prayer. I will ask St. Roch to bring you back soon, and if you don't come I will make a novena for you. When papa was so ill I made one, and good St. Roch cured him."

Together the two children entered the beautiful little ivy-covered chapel, and, with clasped hands and reverent mien, knelt devoutly at the shrine before the youthful figure of St. Roch.

He was Dea's saint, a saint above all others; the beautiful youth, with his faithful dog beside him, who went about in those old days of famine and pestilence, feeding the hungry and nursing the sick. She devoutly believed that he had cured her father, and she also believed that he would bring Philip back safely, if she prayed sincerely. So she knelt there, her head uplifted, her eyes fixed on the face of the youthful saint, while her lips murmured over and over the simple petition, "Good St. Roch, hear us; good St. Roch, pray for us."

And as she prayed, the rosy light streamed down from the stained window above and fell over her, making her as radiant and beautiful as the pictured saint before her. And it was in that attitude, and with that sweet light over her, that Philip always remembered her.

CHAPTER XVI

THE DEPARTURE

AT last they were ready to go. Everything was arranged, all the difficulties overcome, and all the obstacles surmounted. Mr. Ainsworth found it very easy to persuade Philip to leave the "happy family" with Dea; and Lilybel was employed to carry the basket to its destination, where Dea received it joyfully and introduced its lively occupants to the little home on Villeré street. This proved a satisfactory arrangement on both sides. Philip was quite willing to leave these objects of his affection with Dea, and Dea was delighted to have something of Philip's to care for. It was a bond of union between them, and she was sure that it would be a happy one, providing Homo was inclined to share her favor with the puppy and the kitten.

"I think Homo will be good to them," she said hopefully to Philip, "although he is very jealous sometimes; but he knows they are yours, and he's so fond of you that I'm certain he'll let me keep them."

As to the wardrobe, Mrs. Ainsworth had represented to the boy, without wounding his pride, that the little garments he had always worn would be too thin for a colder climate, and that he would outgrow them before he returned, so he had better give them to Lilybel, who would look very well in the best suit. This Philip readily agreed to; he felt that he owed Seline a debt of gratitude for many favors, and in spite of Lilybel's unreliable character, he secretly liked him. Therefore the bag and its contents were transferred to the droll little darky, who carried them off on his head as proudly as though they had been the spoils of a conqueror.

Now they sat in the dismantled studio with the unsettled air of pilgrims about to start forth on a new venture. Mr. Ainsworth, in his traveling outfit, was moving about restlessly. Mrs. Ainsworth appeared tired and worried, while Philip, in his handsome new clothes, did not seem quite as much at his ease, nor look nearly as picturesque as he did in the homely garments he had always worn. Dea was there; she had been with them all day, and they had invited her to remain and go with them in the carriage to the station. Now she sat beside Philip, very quiet and pale; from time to time she looked at him with a mingled expression of admiration and dissatisfaction. He did not seem quite the same boy in these strange new clothes; she could not feel so intimate with him, and there was a little formality in her manner toward him, although her heart was very heavy at the thought of his going. Philip, now that the time had actually come to start on his first journey, was eager to be off. He was pale and excited; suddenly the tears would start to his eyes, but he would wipe them off bravely, while he appeared to busy himself with Père Josef's "children," who, in their outdoor costume, the red-and-yellow handkerchief were quite as impatient as Philip, if one could judge from the flurry and scurry going on within the cage. "They are very lively," said Philip, peeping in at them; "they are playing *Colin-Maillard.*"

Dea smiled a little, but said nothing. She was wondering how they could be so happy at such a time; and Mr. and Mrs. Ainsworth were thinking that the "children" were likely to be something of a nuisance on the journey.

At last the carriage was announced, much to the relief of all, and they started at once for the station. When they arrived there and stepped out on the platform, the first persons they saw were Grande Seline and Lilybel, anxiously awaiting them.

Seline's good, dusky face was full of trouble, and her eyes were suspiciously red. Lilybel, in Philip's best suit, was grinning and rolling his eyes extravagantly, while he balanced on his head a large paper box.

The moment Seline saw Philip, she hurried to him, and took him, new suit, Père Josef's "children" and all, in a broad embrace. "My, my!" she sobbed, "an' yer really is goin' erway, an' so hansum in yer new mournin'! My, my, chile! How yer spects Ma'mselle Dea an' me 's goin' ter live when yer done gone?"

"But I'll be back soon, Seline," said Philip, bravely, as he disengaged himself from the old woman's clasp and wiped her tears off his face; "I'll be back soon—won't I?" and he looked appealingly at Mr. and Mrs. Ainsworth. They nodded an affirmative, and smiled assuringly. "Next winter, if nothing happens," they said.

"An', chile," continued Seline, somewhat comforted by this promise, "I 's done made yer a fine loaf of cake ter take along, 'cause I don't know as yer 'll get cake whar yer goin', an' I 's put some fried chicken in der box, an' a bag full er pralines."

"Oh, thank you, Seline," said Philip; he was not ungrateful for such tangible proofs of good-will.

"Here, Lilybel, jes' let dat gentleman"—indicating the porter—"put dat box in Mars' Philip's seat; an' M'sieur," turning to Mr. Ainsworth, "I hope you an' your madam'll take a bite of dat cake an' chicken."

Mr. and Mrs. Ainsworth thanked Seline heartily, and wished her a kind good-by; then they drew Dea to them and kissed her tenderly. "Don't forget us, my child; we will bring Philip back soon," they whispered.

The last moment had come. It was time for the train to start, and the last good-bys must be said. Philip took Dea's little hand with a tremulous smile and a dry sob; he would not cry then; tears would come later. "I must get on the train now, Dea; but stand right here where I can see you, and don't cry when I'm gone. I'm sure to come back soon." He spoke hurriedly and hopefully. "I've got to come back to bring Père Josef's 'children.' Good-by, Dea." Then he kissed her tremulously. "Good-by. Good-by, Seline. Good-by, Lilybel." And without looking back, pale and excited, he followed Mr. and Mrs. Ainsworth into the waiting car.

Seline put her handkerchief to her eyes and sobbed, Dea hid her face in her hands, and Lilybel sniffed and wiped his eyes on the corner of Seline's apron, and that was the tableau Philip saw as the train rolled out of the station.

When it was nearly gone from sight, Dea looked up. She was very pale and her eyes were quite dry, but her small face was full of sorrow. At that moment she caught a glimpse of Philip; he was leaning bareheaded from the window of the car. Mrs. Ainsworth's arm was around him, the wind blew the curls away from his forehead, he smiled and waved his hand. Then his beautiful boyish face became an indistinct blot; and so Toinette's Philip went away from Dea's sight out into the wide, wide world.

CHAPTER XVII

A LITTLE HEIRESS

TWO elderly ladies sat in a handsome drawing-room of a fine house on Madison Avenue in the city of New York. They were each not far from seventy, but, owing to their rich and fashionable attire, they did not look their years. One was Mrs. Ainsworth, the mother of the artist, the other a friend who had just returned from a long residence abroad.

Mrs. Ainsworth, or Madam Ainsworth as she was always called, because of her having lived a great part of her life in France, was a handsome old lady, tall, stately, and somewhat severe, with an inflexible expression, and clear steel-blue eyes, which seemed to pierce one like gimlets when she looked at one with disfavor. She was left, when quite young, a widow with a large fortune, and three children. Philip, the elder and favorite son, was among the first to enlist at the breaking out of the civil war, and went to the front at twenty-five a captain in his regiment, but never returned from the scene of the conflict; Edward, the artist; and Mary, Mrs. Van Norcom, who was now, like her mother, a rich widow, but with only one child, a daughter, a little heiress to a large fortune in her own right.

The old ladies were talking very rapidly and very earnestly; they had not met for years, yet they had been friends since their school-days, and their conversation was a jangle of reminiscences, histories of family affairs, and the current events of the day.

"And so Mary has gone to Nice for the winter, and left the little heiress with you," said the friend.

"Yes," said Madam Ainsworth, with a sigh. "Poor Mary is a confirmed invalid; the doctor said she must go, and we couldn't expose Lucille to the dangers of a sea voyage and a change of climate. You can't think what a responsibility she is; she is such a frail child, and just think of all that money, if anything should happen to her."

"It goes to some charitable institution if she should not live to be twenty-one, does it not?" asked the visitor.

"Yes, that was John Van Norcom's strange will. Of course he left Mary well provided for, but we should not like all that money to go out of the family, especially when a part of it was originally our money. You know, after dear Philip's death"—here Madam Ainsworth sighed more heavily, as she glanced at a beautiful portrait on the wall of a young man in an officer's uniform—"I divided what would have been his between Edward and Mary. John Van Norcom and Philip were like brothers, and I felt that Philip would want John to have the control of his part. And John managed it well; he made a great fortune by clever investments, and that railroad doubled it."

"I hear Edward has really settled down to an artist's life," remarked the friend.

"Yes. Poor Edward," her voice was quite doleful, "*he* never had any faculty for making money, but an excellent one for spending it; and Laura is a little— just a little—unconventional," she hesitated slightly for the right word; "*she* likes their wandering life. I'm not surprised at *her*, but Edward—where does *he* get the Bohemian taint?"

"Oh, one does not necessarily inherit these tastes; they can be cultivated," replied the friend. "I suppose the loss of their son has unsettled them."

"Yes, it has unsettled their judgment. What do you think they have done, and without consulting *me?*"

"Really, I can't say. What have they done?" asked the friend, leaning forward eagerly.

"Why, my dear, they have *adopted* a boy, and a little waif at that. An orphan of whose parents they know nothing; as nearly as I can find out he was a little street-gamin. Edward sent me a sketch of him, *barefooted*, selling flowers."

"Where did they find him?"

"Oh," with a very bitter sigh, "in the South—of all places. It is like opening an old wound, and, strange to say, the boy's name is Philip. I think the name interested them in the first place, and now Laura is really daft over the child; she is quite foolish about him. Says he is the image of my grandson, who was singularly like *my* poor Philip; that he is charming, handsome, refined, and all that. I think she exaggerates a little; it is not likely that a child of that class could resemble one of *our* family."

"Impossible!" said the friend gravely.

"And the worst part of it is that they will spend the winter with me. You know they have had my house while I was away, and I can't refuse them, as there is plenty of room for us all. In fact, I think they imagine it is their home, they have lived here so much. They have been in the mountains all the autumn, and now they write—I had just read the letter when you came in—that they will be here this evening with *that* boy; and Lucille here for the winter. What am I to do? I really don't want her to have a rough, common boy for a companion. Mary wouldn't like it. It is very annoying. However, I must make the best of it. I must keep Lucille away from him, and I don't think it will be difficult; she is a born aristocrat, and so discriminating for a child of her age. Mary has brought her up so well, and her governess, Mademoiselle d'Alby, is the grand-daughter of a count and *so* elegant; and her maid is the orphan of a poor clergyman and really a lady. The little heiress is surrounded with the best. We will not have any common, ignorant people about her. She is so delicate and sensitive she can't be too carefully shielded."

"I should like to see her," murmured the friend, quite awestricken. "She must be like a little princess."

"She is out taking her airing. I wish you would stay until she returns; she is really worth seeing."

At that moment the door was thrown open by a very dignified servant in a neat livery, and quite a striking group entered. First, a little girl of about eight years dressed in a rich gray velvet coat trimmed with silver-gray fox fur, a broad hat covered with feathers, silk stockings and patent-leather shoes. In one hand, covered with a white chamois-leather glove, she held a small muff on which was fastened a large bunch of lilies-of-the-valley, tied with a broad blue ribbon. She was thin, fair, and slightly freckled, her mouth was wide, her nose tip-tilted, her eyes small and light; but her hair was beautiful—it was a dark auburn, and hung like waves of molten copper over her velvet coat. Behind her walked a stately, middle-aged lady dressed in rich black covered profusely with jet, and bringing up the rear, a sweet-faced, refined looking girl in the white apron and neat cap of a maid. On her arm she carried innumerable wraps of fur and cashmere, and by a broad blue ribbon she led a small French poodle, as white and soft as new fallen snow; he wore an embroidered blanket, and amid the silken hair around his neck sparkled a gold collar set with brilliants, and under his chin, tied with an immense bow of ribbon, was a large bunch of lilies-of-the-valley. The pretty creature was obliged to hold his head well up when he walked, which gave him a ridiculously haughty appearance, while his fastidious little black nose sniffed the air disdainfully.

When Madam Ainsworth saw the child, she went, with the greatest solicitude, to meet her. One would have thought a little princess was making her *entrée*, there was so much ceremony.

"Why, my dear," said the old lady, taking the child's small hand between both of hers, "you are back earlier than usual. Didn't you enjoy your drive? Were you cold? Was 'Fluff' troublesome? I hope Mademoiselle and Helen kept plenty of wraps around you." Then she added, as she led her across the room, "Here is a dear old friend; will you come and speak to her a moment before you go upstairs?"

RETURN FROM HER DRIVE.

The child smiled coldly and reached out a gloved hand. "I am very happy to see you," she said, in a clear, high-pitched voice, and with the composure of a leader of society. "I think I have heard grandmama speak of you; you have just returned from abroad, have you not?"

"Shall I remain until mademoiselle goes to her apartment?" asked the governess.

"Does mademoiselle wish Fluff to stay with her?" asked the maid.

"You may all go. I will come presently," replied the little heiress, with a haughty turn of her head; "and Helen, take Fluff's coat off, and give him a small—a very small piece of biscuit, and just *one* caramel." Then she turned again to the visitor and began a conversation upon the topics of the day with the intelligence and dignity of a grown woman.

When she considered that she had discharged her duty with propriety toward her grandmama's friend, she said a formal good morning, and walked haughtily from the room.

Both old ladies watched her admiringly; then Madam Ainsworth said, "Am I not right? is she not a rare little creature?"

"She's remarkable, she's charming!" replied the friend, warmly. "Such intelligence, so gracious, so lovely! Dear, dear, what a sensation she will make some day!"

CHAPTER XVIII

A Little Waif

MR. AND MRS. AINSWORTH arrived, bag and baggage,—Philip and Père Josef's "children" included,—an hour before dinner, and went directly to their rooms on the third floor. Madam Ainsworth had taken the apartments usually occupied by her son and his wife for the use of the little heiress and her attendants. This innovation did not please Mrs. Ainsworth, and she sighed discontentedly as she mounted the extra flight; and when she saw the small room—little more than a closet—which had been carelessly prepared for Philip, she looked indignantly at her husband and said, in a low voice, "This shows plainly how we shall be received; I wish we had gone to a hotel."

"My dear Laura, mother would never have forgiven us had we done so. Let us make the best of it, and not resent her unkindness. Philip will be very comfortable here, and I like our rooms as well as the lower ones."

Mrs. Ainsworth did not so much object to the change, only that she saw in it an indication that made her anxious and unhappy.

"I dread your mother's seeing Philip," she said, when they were ready for dinner; "if she treats the poor child coldly and severely he will feel it, for I have found out that he has a very sensitive nature. Have you noticed how he shrinks from everything harsh and unpleasant?"

"Don't borrow trouble, my dear," replied Mr. Ainsworth, soothingly; "let the boy make his own way with her, he is so handsome and winning, and then, perhaps, she will see, as I do, his likeness to my brother when he was a child. Why, often this summer when Philip has been with me in the fields and woods I have fancied myself a boy again, so vividly has he brought back the memory of our happy childhood. If mother can only see him as I do, his future is safe. You know Philip was her idol; to her he was simply perfection, but I—*I* was always faulty." And Mr. Ainsworth sighed a little sadly at the memory of past injustices which he had forgiven, but not forgotten.

Madam Ainsworth, in one of her richest gowns, and an unusual quantity of jewelry, was walking impatiently up and down the drawing-room waiting for dinner to be announced.

"As Lucille dines with us, I suppose that little waif must," she thought angrily. "I can't suggest to Laura that he should eat by himself, and his table manners must be dreadful. Really, it is a great trial to have a little beggar thrust on one in this way." Then a new thought struck her, and she started violently. "Dear, dear, I must make my will over; I must make it so that this little waif can't inherit *my* money from Edward. I wonder if they have legally adopted him; I wonder if they could. I must see my lawyer the first thing in the morning."

When Mr. and Mrs. Ainsworth, with Philip between them, entered the drawing-room, they were prepared for a very cold reception. The old lady retreated to her chair and sat upon it as an offended queen might sit upon her throne; her face was severe, her eyes were like points of steel. She allowed her son to kiss her, then turned her cheek, with a cold "How do you do, Laura?" toward her daughter-in-law.

Mr. Ainsworth flushed a little, and his voice was tremulous, as he said, "Mother, this is our adopted son, another Philip; I hope you will love him. My dear boy, this lady is my mother. I'm sure you'll be as fond of her as you are of us."

Philip came forward readily and held out his hand with a friendly smile.

Madam Ainsworth put up her lorgnette and looked at the child steadily and severely; then she reached him the tips of her fingers, while she said sharply, "So this is the new member of your family? Where is the resemblance I've heard so much about? This boy is very brown—*my* grandson was fair."

Philip shrank back as though he had received a blow; instinctively he felt the hostility of the old lady's attitude. He looked surprised and grieved, and his lips were tremulous.

Mrs. Ainsworth put her arm around him protectingly, and said, with unusual tenderness, "Come, my dear, let us look at the pictures while your papa talks with Madam Ainsworth. This," she continued, in a low voice, stopping before the portrait of the young man in an officer's uniform, "is your papa's brother who was killed in the war. Your papa thinks you are like what he was at your age; he told me so before I ever saw you."

In the six months that had passed since Toinette's Philip became Philip Ainsworth, the boy had changed somewhat. The ageing process that had begun with his first sorrow had continued, and now all the chubby infantine look was gone from his face; he was taller and thinner, and his outdoor life among the mountains had browned his rosy skin and added a more mature color to the delicate tint of his cheeks. He was a handsome, manly boy, a little shy at times, but never awkward nor ill-bred; his adoptive parents had never had cause to blush at any rudeness on his part. As far as one could perceive from his deportment, he might have been born to the purple. And, as Mr. Ainsworth had said, he was a child that one could love. To say that he had never regretted his old life would not be true. There had been times through that delightful summer when he had felt a little homesick, a yearning for his mammy and the old garden, a longing for Dea, for Seline, and even Lilybel. At times he pined for the Major and the melodious notes of the Singer; often and often he fancied that he heard among the northern forests a little brown bird twitter "sweety-sweety-sweet." Sometimes he would go away by himself, and lie down under a tree and cry a little, because the voices of nature were strange to him; but he would comfort himself by talking to Père Josef's "children," who were a never-failing source of amusement. "We will go home soon," he would say confidently; "Père Josef will be back. It will be spring, and we will smell the sweet-olive and jasmine." But he never breathed his regrets to any one beside the "children"; he was always bright and happy, because he was always occupied and amused; the newness of a life of ease and luxury had not worn off, and he had not yet felt the restraints of a higher civilization.

While Mrs. Ainsworth and Philip were still looking at the pictures, the little heiress entered followed by her governess. When the boy glanced up at her he thought that she looked like a large doll he had seen one Christmas in a shop-window. Lucille was dressed in a blue silk frock covered with filmy white lace. Like the doll, she wore blue silk stockings, and the neatest little shoes, with narrow straps buttoned around her ankles. In one slender hand she carried the bunch of lilies-of-the-valley that she had worn on her muff during her drive. She had been taught that it was an indication of high breeding to be polite to every one; so, after she had welcomed her uncle and aunt with great formality, she went directly to Philip, and gave him the tips of her fingers, in exactly the manner of her grandmother, as she said, in her little artificial voice, "How do you do? I'm very happy to see you." Then she stood off, and scrutinized him impertinently from under the copper-colored fringe that covered her forehead.

Philip was not in the least disconcerted, but rather amused. It was as if the doll had stepped down from the shop-window and said, "How do you do?" So he began to chatter in the most cordial way, and even felt a desire to pull a strand of the copper-colored hair to see if the doll would resent the liberty; but he restrained himself, because Madam Ainsworth was looking at him severely, and she even frowned at him. She did not like to see the little heiress and the little waif walking out to dinner side by side. "This will never do," she thought; "I sha'n't encourage any intimacy." So she put them at opposite sides of the table.

There is a sort of freemasonry between children which makes them understand each other. In spite of Lucille's haughty airs Philip felt very friendly toward her, and from time to time he looked across the table and smiled at her as she sat in state beside her governess. He thought it very amusing that the fine lady next to her treated her with so much deference, that Helen in her white cap stood behind her chair, and that the stately butler in livery bent almost double when he spoke to her.

Mr. and Mrs. Ainsworth had been living in fashionable hotels all summer, and Philip had become accustomed to formal service and more or less ceremony, but he had never seen anything like this dinner. He could scarcely eat, so busy was he watching the movements of the butler, and the airs of Lucille. When the butler changed his plates, he thanked him audibly, and smiled up in his face, as if he were an old friend; and the butler, although he looked like a wooden man, was thinking to himself, "Pretty little chap. I'd like to smile back at 'im, if I dared." And Philip felt that they were congenial. In fact, so well did he like him, that he tried to be obliging in little ways. He would have assisted him in changing the plates, but Madam Ainsworth looked at him so severely, and the fine lady in the glittering jet frowned so, and even his papa and mamma made little signs of displeasure. He only meant to be kind, but perhaps, after all, he was not behaving quite properly at such a grand dinner. Then he wondered if it was like this every day, and he thought how tired he would get of seeing the butler change the plates so many times. However, he was glad when at last it was over and he was in the drawing-room again. Then he thought of the "children" all alone in his room, and wondered if the red-haired little girl would like to see them; even though she looked like a doll, he was sure she would be pleased with Père Josef's "children." So he watched his chance, and while the elders of the party were looking over some of his papa's sketches, he boldly approached Lucille, and asked her if she would like to see Père Josef's "children."

"Children!" she exclaimed, raising her haughty little head, and looking at him with cold surprise. "Where are they?"

"They're in my room in a cage."

"In a cage! What do you mean? What are they?"

"They are little mice, dear little white mice."

"Mice, little *mice*, oh, oh!" and her voice sounded quite shrill and natural, while her little blue feet were drawn up under her in a trice. "*Mice!* Where?"

"What is it, darling; what has frightened you? She is quite pale; run, Mademoiselle, run for my vinaigrette," cried Madam Ainsworth.

"Oh, grandmama, he says he has them in his room—just think, *mice* in his room, and he wants to bring them here; don't let him bring them here."

"No, no, my darling, he sha'n't. Edward, take that boy away; he has given Lucille a dreadful shock; take him away immediately."

Mr. and Mrs. Ainsworth were almost convulsed with laughter at the absurd scene, and Philip did not understand in the least what had happened, nor why they led him so hastily from the room.

"He has gone now, darling. Do you feel better? Dear me! what a strange boy. I shall have to request your uncle not to bring him into the drawing-room again if he talks about such things as *mice*." Then she added to herself—"But what can one expect of a little waif—a little street-gamin. It is just as I thought; I must keep Lucille away from him."

When Philip reached the door of his room, he turned to Mrs. Ainsworth, and said in a puzzled voice, "Mama, *did* she, or *didn't* she want to see Père Josef's 'children'?"

"She *didn't* want to see them, my dear. She is afraid of them, and you must not speak of them to her again."

Almost as soon as Philip's head touched his pillow he was asleep, and he had a funny little dream. He thought he was showing Père Josef's "children" to the large doll in the shop-window, when suddenly it screamed and drew up its feet; then some one cried, "Run, Mademoiselle; run quick and fetch my vinaigrette, the poor doll has fainted."

CHAPTER XIX

QUASIMODO FURNISHES A CLUE

A FEW mornings after his arrival in New York, Mr. Ainsworth was in his studio busily engaged in finishing his picture for the Academy exhibition. It was the study of Philip and Dea, his little New Orleans models, and it was very natural and charming.

He thought it better in color than anything he had ever done, and he was anxious to have the opinion of a connoisseur, when the door was opened, and the one of all others whom he most wished to see entered briskly. He was a tall, dark man, with a foreign air, and a decidedly foreign accent.

Mr. Ainsworth turned in his chair, and holding all his implements in one hand, held out the other cordially. "Why, Detrava, how are you? The very man I wanted to see. Take a chair, and tell me what you think of this."

"Hard at it, eh! my friend. Something good, I see." And the visitor laid his hat and stick on the table, and leaning over the artist's shoulder looked for some time critically at the picture.

"Excellent, my friend, excellent," he said heartily. "It's admirable in drawing, and there's feeling in it, a natural pose, and the color fine, plastic, and strong. Interesting little subjects, picturesque, very. Where did you pick them up?"

"Oh, in that artist's Eldorado, New Orleans."

"You were there all winter, were you not?"

"Yes, I went to stay a month, and I stayed six."

"You like it then?"

"Very much; an odd old town, drowsy and dull, but full of color, and no end of material for a painter."

"I have always meant to go there. I ought to go; I have a little property there. One of our family settled there many years ago, and made quite a fortune, but the most of it was lost through the war. However, there were

85

none of that branch left to inherit it, and the remnant came to me. I have never been able to sell it, and it's been more trouble than profit. I think I'll go some day and look after it."

"I would, if I were you," returned Mr. Ainsworth. "You would enjoy the place. It's an artist's paradise compared to these busy northern cities."

"Well, what did you pick up there in the way of curios? I'm told that one sometimes happens on a good piece."

"Yes, there are some old Spanish and French things well worth having. I got that cabinet and this chair; rather good, aren't they? Oh, but here is a little curiosity, an example of exquisite modeling." Mr. Ainsworth jumped up with alacrity, and taking Quasimodo from the cabinet he set the remarkable little figure on the table before the visitor. "There! what do you think of that?" he asked, with satisfaction.

Mr. Detrava looked at the little object silently for a moment; then he said in a subdued voice, "I had a brother who did that kind of thing remarkably well. It reminds me of his work." Then he took the little figure from the table to examine it more closely, and on the base he saw engraved, in tiny letters, Victor Hugo *fecit*. "Why, Ainsworth, how strange! Victor Hugo, my brother's name. Who made this!"

"The father of my little model, there," pointing to the picture. "The child was selling them on the street, and I bought it from her. A very sad case, as near as I could find out, the artist was ill, and poor—so wretchedly poor! I bought a number of his things, all subjects from Victor Hugo's works. The little girl was named Dea, and she had an old dog she called Homo. It was really interesting, so original and picturesque."

"See here, Ainsworth," said Mr. Detrava, after a moment of deep thought, "I believe the man who modeled that figure is my brother Victor. I have been looking for him for the past eight years. It was a fancy of my mother's, who was an ardent admirer of the great French writer, to name him Victor Hugo. He was a strange, dreamy character, and from childhood he had this peculiar talent. My father wanted to make a sculptor of him, but he had no ambition. When he was a little over twenty-one he married my sister's governess. You can imagine the result: offended parents on one side, pride and a stubborn will on the other. One fine day, without a word of farewell, he took his wife and started for America, and from that time we lost every trace of him. My father relented, and tried to discover his whereabouts, but he never succeeded. And since my residence in New York, I have spared neither time nor money in my efforts to find him. This is the first clue," with a glance at Quasimodo, "and I think it will lead to something."

"I am sure it will," returned Mr. Ainsworth. "Everything agrees. The artist in wax came from France about eight years ago. The child was named Dea for her mother. Her father's name is Victor Hugo; he doubtless dropped his last name. I think there can be no doubt. I feel confident that he is your brother."

"And you say he is poor, miserably poor—and ill—and I have plenty. I must start at once and follow this clue. Can you give me directions, so that I can find him when I reach New Orleans."

"He lives on Villeré street; I never heard the number, but I think I know how you can find it," replied Mr. Ainsworth. Then he told Mr. Detrava about Seline. "If you can find the old woman, she will assist you, and possibly Dea might be with her. I am sure there will be no difficulty when you are once there."

After Mr. Detrava had written all the directions very carefully in his memorandum book, he examined the picture again with a great deal of interest.

"What a delicate, sweet-faced child! poor little thing, how hard it has been for her! If I find her, and she is my brother's child, I mean to take care of her for the future. I feel interested in her already. How lucky that I happened in here this morning, Ainsworth! I intended to start for Paris next week, instead I shall start for New Orleans. I can't rest until I know. So good-by, my friend, I shall see your artist's paradise sooner than I expected, and I trust my journey won't be in vain."

"Good-by, and good luck," replied Mr. Ainsworth heartily, and as Mr. Detrava reached the door he added: "If you remain in New Orleans all winter you may see me there. If nothing happens I intend to be there when the jasmine and orange-trees are in bloom."

"Ah, well, we may meet there, then. *Au revoir*, my friend, and not good-by."

CHAPTER XX

AN INNOCENT MISTAKE

ONE day the little heiress came home from dancing-school in a very bad humor, even though her governess had told her that it was exceedingly ill-bred to show temper, no matter how provoking the circumstances might be.

After much serious consideration, Madam Ainsworth had consented to allow Philip to attend dancing-school in the company of Lucille and her governess. "I don't do it because I wish to," she said confidentially to Mademoiselle. "Mrs. Ainsworth asked me whether the boy might go with Lucille, and she is so foolishly fond of him that I did not like to hurt her feelings by refusing, but you must be very discreet, Mademoiselle, you must not allow them to become too friendly, and if the boy is forward or in the least rude, you have my full authority to reprove him."

"I understand perfectly, Madam," replied the governess, with great dignity. "I can assure you I shall do my duty."

"It is surprising to me," continued Madam Ainsworth in a vexed tone, "that the boy is so little impressed with my grand-daughter's position. I don't think he in the least understands that she is his superior, or he would treat her with more deference."

Madam Ainsworth had guessed the truth. Philip did not consider Lucille his superior in any way. In fact, he had never taken the little heiress seriously; to him she was always the over-dressed doll, the dainty little puppet, rather than a real flesh and blood child. Often he would stand with his hands behind him, looking her over, curiously, his blue eyes full of amusement, while the haughty little creature chafed and fumed under his laughing scrutiny. Sometimes he would be possessed with a spirit of mischief, when suddenly he would shock and vex her beyond endurance by taking the most unwarrantable liberties with her poodle, such as standing him on his head, or tying his huge bow on his fluffy little tail. And even the dignified little lady almost relaxed into a smile, when, one day, the small animal jumped into the carriage, just as she was starting for her drive, with a pair of her grandmama's spectacles fastened securely over his big black eyes, and the silky fringe that covered his face drawn back and tied in a stiff bunch on the top of his tiny head, which made him look ridiculously old and wise. Lucille quickly suppressed the involuntary smile, and scornfully remarked that Philip was an ill-bred boy, while mademoiselle frowned severely and muttered something in French that sounded like "*mauvais sujet.*"

Then Philip, laughing merrily, would run to his room to tell the children that he had made the doll angry, or if he met the old butler, he would even slyly whisper it to him.

"Bless me, Master Philip, my boy," the old man would say, chuckling to himself, "'ow you do play tricks on the young lady. If I was you I wouldn't darst for the life of me to take no liberties with 'er; she looks so 'igh an' mighty an' that Frenchwoman 'olds 'er 'ead like one of the royalty."

"Don't you tell any one, Mr. Butler,"—Philip mistook that respectable title of servitude for the old man's name,—"and some day I'm going to get even with Lucille. I've got a plan—I just want to hear her scream again like she did that night when I told her about Père Josef's 'children.' It was so funny."

The old man muttered something about "a hawful little pickle," and went off grinning.

On this day, when Lucille came from dancing-school, in such a temper that even the gentle Helen was made aware of it by some very haughty orders, she went directly to her grandmama's room.

Madam Ainsworth was writing, but she instantly laid down her pen, and looked with dismay at the flushed, angry face of the little heiress.

"Why, my darling," she began, "what has happened?"

"It's that insufferable boy, grandmama. I really cannot endure him."

"Why, why, what? He hasn't dared to be rude. has he?"

"No, not exactly rude, but so stupid—so stupid as to tell all about himself; he mortified me extremely; he made me ashamed of him. It was *so* humiliating, and before Gladys Bleeker, too."

"What did he do, Lucille? What did he say?" and Madam Ainsworth's voice shook with indignation.

"It was so unnecessary. We were standing together, Gladys and I, waiting for a cotillon to be formed, when Philip came up, and I was foolish enough to introduce him to her as *my* cousin. Only think, my cousin! But just then he appeared so nice that I was not ashamed of him. Gladys was holding a bunch of violets, and suddenly he took them from her, and looked at them as if he would devour them. Then he said loud enough for every one to hear: 'I like violets; I used to sell lots of them in New Orleans.'

"'Why, what do you mean?' asked Gladys. '*You* used to sell violets? Why, you must be jesting!'

"'No I'm not,' he replied. 'I used to sell flowers on Rue Royale. I made plenty of money for Mammy.'

"Gladys laughed, and looked at me so spitefully. Oh, grandmama, I thought I should faint. I was quite overcome for a moment. It was *so* dreadful, when I had just introduced him as my cousin."

"It *was*, my dear. What a shocking boy he is," said Madam Ainsworth, bitterly. "It's just what I expected. And to think of *your* being annoyed by such a common little waif. I'm afraid you'll be ill. You are so excited, so nervous. But don't fret, darling. Perhaps, after all, Gladys thought he was jesting."

"No, no, grandmama. I'm sure she thought he was speaking the truth. I was so shocked that I couldn't stay to finish my lesson. I had Mademoiselle bring me home directly; and, really—really, I can't go again with that ill-bred boy."

"You shall not, my dear. I will speak to your aunt. He must not be allowed to go anywhere with you. He must not distress you in this way."

An hour later Madam Ainsworth and her daughter-in-law had a rather unpleasant interview, which resulted in the termination of Philip's dancing lessons.

"He should be punished severely, Laura," insisted Madam Ainsworth. "He should not be allowed to distress Lucille in this way. He has made the poor child quite ill. He certainly should be punished."

"But how can I punish him for simply telling the truth," pleaded Mrs. Ainsworth. "He did not know that there was any impropriety in his telling the truth."

"He should be taught that the truth is not to be spoken at all times," returned Madam Ainsworth, decidedly.

"Oh, I could not make him understand *that!* Truthfulness is his great virtue. He is so frank, so honest, he would see only deception and falsehood where a more mature mind would discriminate. I would not for worlds confuse his impressions of right and wrong. His ideas are so simple and clear on those points that it would be cruel to change them."

"Very well. Since you approve of his annoying Lucille, he cannot be allowed to go out with her."

"Lucille should not have been annoyed by his innocent remark," returned Mrs. Ainsworth, coldly. "And as to his going out with her, that is entirely as you wish. I can keep him away from dancing-school, but I cannot punish him for telling the truth."

CHAPTER XXI

THE POOR DOLL FAINTS

AS the winter passed away, and the days of early spring approached, Philip began to show signs of restlessness, and anxiety for a change. Mr. Ainsworth had spoken of going South in March, and Philip counted away the weeks until that usually rude month, coming in like a lamb instead of the traditional lion, brought soft sunshine, with a hint of spring on the air.

One day when Philip was taking his lesson in drawing, for he had begun a regular course of study early in the winter, and was making such rapid progress that Mr. Ainsworth was delighted, he looked up suddenly and said, with a touch of anxiety in his voice: "Shall we start soon now, papa? It's March; and you said we should go in March."

"Why, Philip, aren't you contented here? I'm sure it's very pleasant. I don't feel like going while this fine weather lasts."

"But, papa, it's time for Père Josef to be back, and I *must* be home when he gets back."

"Why is it so imperative that you should be there as soon as he is?"

"Because I have his 'children,' and I must take them to him. He only left them with me while he was gone, and it would not be right to keep them after he gets back. And then, there is something I want to ask him."

"What is it, Philip? What do you want to ask him?"

"About my father and mother. Mammy said he would tell me. And she said he had some papers for me."

"Really! did she tell you that!" exclaimed Mr. Ainsworth, excitedly. "Why didn't you let me know of that before, Philip?"

"I didn't think of it, papa. And it wouldn't have been any use while he was away. But now if he's back, I want to see him awfully, to ask him that question."

"So do I, my dear boy. I will write to the priest at St. Mary's—Père Martin, isn't he called? He can tell me if Père Josef has returned, or where a letter will reach him."

"Yes, Père Martin will know," replied Philip, eagerly. "And can't you ask him about Dea?" he added, softly. "I'm anxious about Dea. I'm afraid her money is all gone, and that she can't sell any of her father's little figures. I want to go back to help her."

"My dear, I have some good news for you from Dea," said Mr. Ainsworth, smiling tenderly, as he looked at the boy's flushed, earnest face. "I wanted to let your mama know first—it makes her so happy to tell you pleasant things; but I won't keep you waiting. I had a letter this morning from Mr. Detrava. You remember I told you about my friend, who started some time ago for New Orleans, with the idea that Dea's father was his brother, for whom he had been searching a long time. Well, he was right. The artist in wax is Victor Hugo Detrava, the only brother of my friend—and heir with him to a handsome fortune in France. So Dea is well provided for, her uncle is unmarried, and from his letter I can tell that he is charmed with his lovely little niece."

Philip's face was a study of various emotions, surprise and joy predominating, while he listened to Mr. Ainsworth. "I'm so glad that Dea has some one to take care of her," he exclaimed, when the artist had finished his pleasant story. "And she is rich! Now she can buy her father all the books he wants, how happy she will be! I wish I could see her to tell her how glad I am."

"You shall, my dear Philip. If Père Josef is back we shall start for the South within a week or two."

Philip was in the highest spirits. To be back in his old home, to see Dea and Père Josef—oh, it was delightful to think of. He laughed and chattered incessantly, and was so excited over the good news that he could hardly attend to his lesson. He had not been happy lately. Since the dancing-school episode, Madam Ainsworth had treated him so severely, and Lucille had looked at him so disdainfully, that he knew he had offended them seriously, though in what way he could not imagine. They surely could not be so angry with him for his harmless pranks with the poodle. However, he did not care now; he was going away from them—he was going home, and he was so merry that Lucille was more indignant than ever. She felt that he was not in the least sorry for humiliating her in the presence of Gladys Bleeker—who, although she pretended to be her friend, was really her enemy, for she had repeated Philip's indiscreet remark to every girl in dancing-school. Therefore, each time she went to take her lesson, she returned home in a very disagreeable humor, and Philip had to bear her contemptuous airs as he best could.

"It's no use," he thought to himself; "she won't ever like me, and she treats me worse than she does Fluff. I've got to get even with her. I've got to have some fun before I go."

"LUCILLE WAS SCRAMBLING ON TO THE HALL TABLE."

One day, when she returned from her airing, very much excited because Gladys Bleeker had bowed coldly to her when they met in the park, Philip was in the butler's pantry alone, huddled behind the partly closed door, with an air of great secrecy. Suddenly a piercing shriek came from the hall—not one, but a succession of shrill screams, which filled the house and brought Madam Ainsworth to the head of the stairs, pale and trembling with terror. Mademoiselle had jumped on a chair, and was holding her skirts up in a most undignified position, while Lucille was scrambling on to the hall table, her hair and feathers in the wildest disorder, her eyes wide with fear, while from her parted lips issued cries which might have been heard a block away.

The only brave one of the party seemed to be the maid, Helen, who was pursuing a tiny white object gliding along at the other side of the hall, and which she was trying to belabor with an umbrella. But her efforts were in vain; she could not hit it, it slipped away and disappeared through a narrow opening in the door of the butler's pantry.

"What is it—what is the matter? Lucille, darling, are you hurt?" cried Madam Ainsworth half-way down-stairs.

"The mice, the white mice," shrieked Lucille. "They're in the hall, they're running all over the floor. Oh, oh, I'm so afraid!"

"*Les souris, les petites souris, elles sont partout,*" added Mademoiselle hysterically, as she drew her skirts closer around her.

"Where are they? Oh, where are they? Are they running up the table legs?" cried Lucille, fairly dancing with terror.

"*Sont-elles sous la chaise?*" gasped Mademoiselle.

"They're gone," cried the victorious Helen, flourishing the umbrella. "They ran into the butler's pantry."

"Shut the door quickly before they get out," called Madam Ainsworth, as she rushed to Lucille and clasped her nervously. "My dear, my darling! oh, oh, you are faint! Run and get my vinaigrette. Quick! quick! fetch some water; the poor child is unconscious," cried the old lady, as Lucille—furs, feathers, and all—tumbled, a limp bundle, into her grandmama's arms.

Yes, the poor doll had really fainted; after all, she was a frail little creature. There was a terrible commotion; she was laid, pale and crumpled, on the drawing-room sofa; and the coachman, who was at the door, was despatched for the doctor.

Philip, not dreaming of such a tragic ending to his little comedy, felt as guilty as an assassin, as he stuffed a small white object into his pocket and hurriedly wound up a long black thread.

He was terribly frightened at the result of his effort to get even with Lucille. He felt that he had surpassed himself, and without waiting to know the awful consequences of his practical joke, scuttled away to his room, where he threw himself on his bed laughing and crying at the same time.

When the little heiress had somewhat recovered,—which was very soon, and long before the doctor arrived,—Bassett walked gravely into the drawing-room, his face as placid and impenetrable as a mask, and calmly asked what had happened.

"Why, they went into your pantry, Bassett," said Madam Ainsworth, excitedly. She was kneeling by the sofa rubbing the thin hands of the child, who had revived very suddenly from her unconscious condition, and was sitting up sipping a cordial from a tiny glass.

"What, Madam? What went into my pantry?" asked Bassett, rubbing his hands, with a puzzled expression.

"Why, the mice. Helen saw them run in there, and *you* must have seen them."

"I didn't see nothing in my pantry, an' I've just come from there. If you'll allow me to say it, madam, there's some mistake."

"What! Do you mean to say that they didn't go in there—that boy's white mice, that he turned loose into the hall on purpose to frighten Miss Van Norcom?"

"Bless me! no, Madam. Master Philip's white mice never put a foot in my pantry."

"I saw them, or I'm sure I saw *one;* perhaps it was only one," said Helen, her bright eyes twinkling with mischief.

"I saw them running all over the floor," declared the governess, emphatically.

"Oh! I saw them climbing up the table-legs," wailed Lucille.

"If you'll permit me, Madam, I'll venture to say that them little hinnocent hanimals of Master Philip's hain't never been out of their cage."

"How dare you say such a thing, Bassett? Do you suppose that Miss Van Norcom and the others are mistaken?" exclaimed Madam Ainsworth, sharply.

"By no means, Madam. If I may be allowed to suggest, perhaps hit was what is called han hoptical hillusion," returned the old man, blandly.

"Nonsense, Bassett! It was that troublesome boy's mischief. It is getting unendurable."

"Will you hallow me to go to Master Philip's room, Madam? If the little hanimals are not there in their cage, I'll hadmit that they are 'id in my pantry," and Bassett bowed and marched out as gravely as he had marched in.

In a few moments he returned with an unmistakable look of triumph on his placid face. "Hit's just as I hexpected, Madam. Them little hanimals are 'uddled hup together, sound asleep in their cage; and Master Philip is there 'ard at work a-studyin' of 'is Latin."

"It is certainly very strange," said Madam Ainsworth, looking mystified; "but I am not convinced. You can go to your pantry, Bassett; and when Miss Van Norcom is better I will investigate the matter."

Bassett bowed very low, and went out with a little spring in his step, and a merry twinkle in his dull old eyes. "Bless my 'eart." he muttered as he closed the pantry door, and gave a long sigh of relief. "I've saved the little pickle this time; 'e's safe if my young lady's young lady don't peach. She sees 'ow it is, an' she's too good to blow on the pretty little chap, so I think 'e's safe to get out of a bad scrape."

CHAPTER XXII

PHILIP PLEADS FOR THE "CHILDREN"

AFTER dinner Mr. and Mrs. Ainsworth and Philip were alone in the drawing-room. The doctor came and spoke lightly of Lucille's ill turn, prescribed a simple sedative, and went away smiling to himself at Madam Ainsworth's highly colored description of the dreadful shock his little patient had received. She had been put to bed, and her grandmother would not leave her even to take her dinner; and as mademoiselle was required to be in constant attendance, there was no one at the table but the three who were now together in the drawing-room. Mr. Ainsworth was looking troubled, Mrs. Ainsworth annoyed, and Philip strangely subdued. The boy's high spirits had vanished, he was pale, and there was a suspicion of tears about his eyes; he was trying to read, but from time to time he glanced furtively from Mr. to Mrs. Ainsworth, who were discussing the event of the afternoon.

"It is absurd the way Lucille is encouraged in her silly fancies," said Mrs. Ainsworth, with some irritation in her voice.

"But it was not only Lucille, my dear; they all say they saw *something*," returned Mr. Ainsworth, warmly. "They could not all be mistaken. They could not all be the victims of 'han hoptical hillusion,' as Bassett says. Helen declares that *she* saw something, and Helen is not one to indulge in nerves."

"I don't know. I can't explain it. I only know Philip had nothing to do with it, nor the 'children,' either." said Mrs. Ainsworth, decidedly. "I was in Philip's room just before the outcry, and the little creatures were asleep in their cage, just as Bassett said. It is so unreasonable of your mother to suppose that Philip would let the mice out, and risk losing them, just to frighten Lucille."

"Mama, may I go to my room?" asked Philip, coming forward for his good-night kiss.

"Certainly, my dear, if you wish to. You look pale. Aren't you well?"

"I'm well, thank you, mama; but—but I'm tired."

"Don't be unhappy, my dear, about this foolish affair. I'm sure we shall be able to convince Madam Ainsworth, when she is calmer, that *you* had nothing to do with it."

Philip hesitated a moment, with an appealing look at Mrs. Ainsworth, and then kissing her again, with much warmth, he went out silently.

The two remained in deep thought for some time. Then Mr. Ainsworth said, with conviction: "Philip knows more about this than we think he does. I can tell by his manner that he has something on his mind."

"My dear, you are becoming strangely like your mother, with your absurd suspicions!" exclaimed Mrs. Ainsworth. "How could the mice be asleep in their cage and running about the hall at the same time? I'm not surprised at your mother's unreasonableness. She dislikes the poor boy, and takes every means of showing it by her unkind accusations. But for *you* to suspect Philip! You, who know how truthful he is!"

"Did he *say* he knew nothing about it?" asked Mr. Ainsworth, cautiously.

"I did not ask him. I would not hurt him so much as to have him think that I doubted his word. All he said was that the mice were not out of their cage; and I know he spoke the truth."

"Well, Laura, we won't discuss it any more. But if I find that Philip is keeping anything back, I shall be greatly disappointed in him, for he's not the boy I thought he was."

"There is no reason why he should keep anything back," rejoined Mrs. Ainsworth, firmly—determined to defend him to the last. "He is very brave, and not at all afraid to tell the truth. He is always willing to bear the consequences of his little pranks. He is never malicious—only mischievous— and where others would laugh at his harmless tricks, your mother treats them as if they were crimes. If you listen to your mother, she will succeed in turning *you* against the poor little fellow. Even now, I think you have changed toward him. He does not interest you as he did."

"Now, my dear, *you* are unjust. I have not changed; I love Philip dearly, but I am not blind to his faults, and I do think he is a little—just a little—malicious toward Lucille. Wouldn't it be better to speak to him gently, and request him not to play any more practical jokes on that nervous, foolish child? Mother is so displeased, it will end in trouble between us if it goes on, and you must see how unpleasant that would be."

"If I should reprove Philip, it would be treating the matter seriously; and it would be equivalent to admitting that I doubted his word. It would be a repetition of the dancing-school affair, and I am not disposed to make mountains out of mole-hills. The only thing for us to do is to take the boy away as soon as possible. We can never be happy here with him; your mother's dislike to him is unaccountable." And Mrs. Ainsworth got up and paced the floor, flushed and indignant.

"Don't excite yourself, Laura dear," said Mr. Ainsworth; "as soon as we hear that the priest is back we will start for New Orleans, and we may learn something from him about the boy that will relieve us of all responsibility."

Mrs. Ainsworth said no more, but she felt very dissatisfied and unhappy. Already her assumed duties were pressing rather heavily upon her, and for the first time she regretted that they had been so hasty—that they had not considered more seriously the importance of the step they had taken.

The next morning, quite early, Madam Ainsworth heard a timid knock at her door; and on opening it she was surprised to see Philip standing there very pale but very resolute. It was the first time that he had intruded upon the privacy of her apartment, and she felt that the visit betokened something of importance.

The boy's blue eyes were timid and appealing, although his lips were firm, his shoulders erect, and his manly little figure full of courage. "If you please, Madam, may I come in? I want to tell you something," he said in a very gentle, subdued voice.

"Certainly, come in," replied Madam Ainsworth, coldly. "I'm very busy this morning, but I will listen to what you have to say"; and she seated herself with dignity at her writing-table, and began opening her letters with a business-like air.

"I want to tell you about yesterday," said Philip, his face crimsoning and his lips quivering. "It wouldn't be right not to tell you. I would have told last night only for Mr. Butler. I don't want you to blame him; he wasn't to blame, he didn't know about it. I hid behind his pantry door, when he was out. He didn't even help me make *it;* he never saw it. You won't blame him, will you?" and Philip looked imploringly into the severe face before him.

"Oh, Bassett was not an accomplice, then?" said Madam Ainsworth, a touch of sarcasm in her voice.

"He didn't know until after it was done. But he said he would stand by me. I don't mind for myself. You can punish me *good*. But poor Mr. Butler Bassett—I like him, and I don't want him punished."

"Oh! I see; you are great friends," said the old lady, grimly. "Well, go on with your interesting developments. I don't in the least understand what contemptible tricks you were up to."

Philip winced a little; but he pulled himself together, determined to tell the whole truth. "Why, you see, Lucille was so cross to me that I wanted—I wanted to pay her off. I wanted to frighten her. But I didn't want to make her ill. I wouldn't hurt her for the world. I wouldn't hurt any girl, even if she did—even if she did *curl her lip at me*. So I just thought it would be fun to make something like a mouse run across the floor."

"Then there was something!" exclaimed Madam Ainsworth, triumphantly.

"Yes, there was. They did see something; but it wasn't one of the 'children.'"

"What was it?" asked the old lady, impatiently.

"Why, it was a mouse; but not a live mouse. I made it out of wool, and put on a little tail of tape, and the two eyes were jet beads off of Mademoiselle's fringe. I tied a long black thread to it, and put it in the hall just where Lucille would see it when she came in; and I made it jump quickly, by jerking the thread; and when I had frightened them well, I pulled it into the pantry. Helen tried to kill it with the umbrella; but she couldn't get a lick at it. Then Lucille fainted, and Mr. Butler came in and told me to run up the back stairs. So you see that was why I said it wasn't one of the 'children.'" And Philip drew a long breath of relief, now that he had unburdened his conscience, and waited timidly for the result of his confession.

"Really, really! What—what deception!—what falsehood!" exclaimed Madam Ainsworth, angrily. "And Edward has boasted of the boy's truthfulness!"

"It wasn't a falsehood," returned Philip, proudly. "I never tell lies. It was only a—a mistake. It was because I went in Mr. Butler's pantry, and I didn't want him blamed. That's why I didn't tell at first. I'm very sorry now that I did it. I'm very sorry that it made Lucille ill. And I came to ask you to forgive me."

"Forgive you! Indeed, I shall do nothing of the kind. I shall insist on your being punished severely. You must be taught that you can't trifle in this way with me," said Madam Ainsworth, indignantly.

"Well, I don't mind," replied Philip, bravely. "You can punish me. Only please don't blame Mr. Butler."

"I shall settle with Bassett at my leisure. And I shall order him to take those nasty little vermin out of the house immediately."

"What vermin? You don't mean Père Josef's 'children,' do you?" asked Philip, in a horrified voice. "They're not vermin. They're just as good and quiet—and they're neat, too! I keep their cage as clean as can be. Oh, you don't mean that they must go?"

"I certainly do. I have had enough trouble since you brought the horrid little things here. I shall give the order to have them taken away at once. I don't care what becomes of them." And Madam Ainsworth turned toward her table as if she had settled the matter definitely.

"Oh, Madam, *please* don't send them away. I can't let them go. Père Josef left them in my care. Oh, please, please don't!" And Philip, in an agony of entreaty, laid his hand on Madam Ainsworth's arm and looked into her face imploringly.

"It's no use to make a fuss. I will not allow them to stay in my house; that is final. Now you may go. I'm too busy to be troubled with such nonsense." And the indignant old lady shook off the little hand angrily.

Poor Philip! he had never dreamed of such a dreadful punishment; he was desperately in earnest now, and, entirely overcome by fear and sorrow, he burst into tears, and clasping his hands passionately, made a last, most pathetic appeal.

"They're so little! They don't know any one but me; they'll be afraid of strangers; they may starve, they may get lost, and they can't find their way home, and what will Père Josef say when he sees me if I don't bring his 'children' back? I promised to take care of them, and I can't if you send them away. I love them so; they are so little and cunning, and they love me. They're all I've got to care for. Don't send them away; please don't! We're going home soon; please let them stay with me till we go! Oh, please do, and I'll be so grateful. I'll try to be good; I won't tease Lucille again. I'll be so glad if you'll let them stay!"

Suddenly Madam Ainsworth started from her chair and looked at the boy almost in terror. Something in his pitiful, pleading voice pierced her to the heart. It was a note of childish sorrow that she had heard long ago, and it softened her instantly. Hot tears sprang to her eyes, and for a moment she could not regain her self-control. At length she said, in a voice that trembled in spite of her effort to make it sound harsh:

"There, there, child!—that will do. Don't go on as if you were insane. If your heart is so set on those horrid little creatures, keep them, and oblige me by never speaking of them again. Now wipe your eyes and go to your room, and in the future try to treat Lucille properly."

"Oh, thank you, thank you!" cried Philip, rapturously, a sudden smile breaking over his face, like a ray of sunlight in the midst of rain. "I'll never forget how good you are, and you won't blame Mr. Butler, will you?" he added, anxiously.

"I'll consider it," she said. "He deserves to be reproved, but for your sake I may overlook his fault." Madam Ainsworth had never before spoken so gently to the boy. At that moment she longed to take him in her arms and hold him to her heart, but she allowed him to leave the room without any further indication of favor. The proud old soul felt that she had made concessions enough for one day, so she resolutely held herself in check—only thinking as her eyes followed the happy little fellow: "It certainly is very strange. The boy quite unnerved me. I really felt for a moment as though he belonged to *me*."

CHAPTER XXIII

ANOTHER RIVAL

MARCH came and went, and Mr. Ainsworth did not go south. After hearing from Père Martin that Père Josef had not returned, and was, as far as he could learn, in the interior of New Mexico, the artist felt that there was no hurry, as a letter might not reach the priest for months. So he lingered in his pleasant studio until April grew old, and verdant young May took her place.

Philip was bitterly disappointed, although he made no complaint. However, it was more bearable because Père Josef was not there, and Dea did not need him. His mind was relieved of its anxieties, and he could wait more patiently. Besides, life to him was pleasanter than it had been: Madam Ainsworth was less severe since the confession, and at times almost kind, and Lucille was less disdainful to him. Still their relations were not at all cordial.

On the day when the little heiress caused such a commotion by fainting at the sight of a wool mouse, Philip understood that she was *not* a doll, but that she was a frail little girl made of the most delicate and fragile clay, and as fine and transparent as a soap-bubble that a breath of wind could blow away. That absurd little scene had taught him several important things. First, that a little heiress may be more refined and sensitive than is a child of poverty, and that what are precious treasures to the humble are very offensive to the "'igher classes" (quoting from Bassett); that a little waif must never try to "get even" with a little aristocrat unless he wants to experience serious defeat; that there are the proud and the meek, and that the proud, instead of the meek, inherit the earth; that the kingdom of the meek is not of this world; that a life of simple, honest poverty is very different from a life of wealth and fashion, and that among the worldly, things are not called by the same names, or judged by the same standards, as they are among the children of nature.

All these contradictions in life became slowly apparent to the intelligent mind of the boy. He had never thought of such things with Toinette and Père

Josef, but now living seemed a very different and much more complicated condition than it had then. Philip was a child of nature, but he was also something of a little philosopher; he could see neither necessity nor reason in some of the ceremonious usages around him. They amused him and made him sad at the same time: such as Bassett holding open the door and bowing so humbly when Madam Ainsworth entered; or of changing the plates a dozen times at dinner; or of taking off one handsome suit of clothes to put on another just to dine in. He could not understand why his fine slippers were not just as good to wear in the drawing-room as were his patent-leather shoes, or why every one stood up until Madam Ainsworth was seated, nor the reason of various other little formalities which Mrs. Ainsworth told him indicated good breeding.

He believed in being polite to every one, even to the servants; in being strictly truthful, obedient, and generous—Toinette had taught him all those things; in emptying his pockets for a beggar where Lucille would refuse a dime; of taking the part of an oppressed small boy, or a hungry, weak dog; of feeding any starving cat in the neighborhood, and strewing the window-sills with crumbs for the freezing sparrows; of taking off his hat when he spoke to a woman; of offering his seat promptly to any one who stood in a public conveyance; of carrying a baby or a basket for a weary mother, or doing any kindness prompted by a noble, sweet nature.

But it was not always right in this fashionable world to follow the promptings of his own heart. At almost every turn he was reproved and repressed for what appeared to him a trivial thing; and this moral pruning and training had set him to thinking seriously. He rebelled secretly against this hothouse culture. Like the vines in his old sunny garden, he wanted to climb to heaven free and untrammeled. He grew pale and thoughtful, and began to look old for his age; he was not developing well under the influence of this over-civilization.

When the trees budded in May, and the grass grew green in the park, he brightened visibly. Every spare moment was spent there; he liked to get away by himself and to brood in the green shadows. He thought much of his past, and he lived over and over the old days that now seemed farther away than ever. His disappointment was deeper than any one guessed. He had trusted implicitly in Mr. Ainsworth's promise to take him home in March, and the easy way in which it was evaded shook his confidence for the first time.

"How do I know," he thought, "that they will ever take me back? Perhaps I shall never see Dea again, or Père Josef, and the poor 'children' may have to stay here always." But after awhile his disappointment wore off; the beauties of the park consoled him—the cool, shady spots, the sunny slopes, and the birds—yes, these strange birds came to him; he had not lost his power of wooing these children of the air. They were unknown to him by name; they were not so rich of plumage nor so sweet of song as his southern friends, but he loved them and welcomed them. Already they knew his peculiar whistle, and would come at his call, to fly down to him and hover about him fearlessly.

Often on sunny afternoons in June, when Madam Ainsworth and Lucille were driving through the shady avenues of the park, they would see Philip lying at full length under a tree, his hat thrown aside, his hair tangled, his face flushed and happy, unmindful of the throng of human beings who might pause to gaze at him as he watched his feathered friends flutter and circle about him.

"HE LIKED TO BROOD IN THE GREEN SHADOWS."

"I think the boy must have gipsy blood in him; just see how uncivilized he looks!" Madam Ainsworth would exclaim indignantly.

"I hope he won't see us and recognize us before all these people," Lucille would say, as she turned her haughty little head in another direction, and shrugged her shoulders disdainfully.

There was no danger of his recognizing them. Philip saw nothing but his blue sky, his birds, and his green trees; or perhaps his thoughts were hundreds of miles away. Again he was Toinette's Philip, setting out pansies in the old garden, while the Major and the Singer fluttered around him; or he was kneeling in the little chapel near the shrine of St. Roch, with Dea beside him, in the sweet rosy light, while she whispered her simple prayer: "Good St. Roch, hear us; good St. Roch, pray for us!"

Sometimes he would hide his face in the grass, and shed a few silent tears because those dear places were so far away that there was nothing left him but the memory of them.

Early in July, Mrs. Van Norcom returned from abroad, and took the little heiress and her attendants away with her to Newport. Shortly after Madam Ainsworth followed, and Mr. and Mrs. Ainsworth and Philip were left alone in the great, silent house. Mr. and Mrs. Ainsworth did not intend to neglect their adopted son, but Mrs. Ainsworth was not well, and was confined the most of the time to her room, and Mr. Ainsworth spent his leisure hours in his wife's company, for her indisposition forced them to remain in the city. And this was another disappointment to Philip, who hoped again to see the forests and mountains where he had passed the previous summer.

However, he had the "children," the park, his drawing, and his books, although he was not so fond of the latter as he should have been. The tutor whom he had during the winter said his pupil was very intelligent and obedient, but he did not like to study, he did not like Latin and mathematics. The tutor feared Philip would always be deficient in those useful branches of learning.

Nature was Philip's favorite book, and art and poetry the mental food be preferred; dry and abstruse studies wearied and disheartened him, and he was glad when his tutor went away for the summer, and left him free to spend his days as he pleased.

Sometimes he would smuggle the "children" out for a holiday, and the genuine pleasure he took in displaying their accomplishments to all the little ragamuffins in the park fully repaid him for the risk he ran. Mr. Ainsworth had objected to his taking them out; he did not like to see the boy surrounded by a crowd of gamins, exhibiting his white mice.

"He looks like a little vagrant," he would say discontentedly to his wife. "When he is with that class of children he seems to become one of them. It is astonishing how many such traits develop in him from day to day. Sometimes I am afraid that he is deteriorating."

"He is growing older," Mrs. Ainsworth would return with a sigh. "The charm of infancy is gone, and he is in the transition state between child and boy,—hardly an interesting age; but in spite of his little faults, he has a beautiful nature. I hope we shall be able to do our duty by him, but sometimes I have serious misgivings. I am doubtful about the wisdom of trying to substitute a strange child in the place of one's own flesh and blood."

"Well, it's too late to think of that now, Laura. It seemed best when we did it, and we must not shirk the responsibility. We can't always control our feelings, but we can always *do* right." And so the conversation ended without the satisfaction that they had come to any decision on a subject that was more or less troublesome.

Early in September, another rival came to take the place of Lucille, and in many respects a more formidable one than the little heiress. Mrs. Ainsworth had a fine little boy; he was named Edward for his father, and his appearance was hailed with great joy. Madam Ainsworth hurried from Newport. An elderly French nurse was engaged, and the little stranger was installed in Lucille's apartment with all the ceremony due to an heir of the Ainsworths.

When Philip first saw the child, he turned quite pale, and his eyes were wet with tears as he stooped and kissed the pink cheeks tenderly, and said, with a smile, "He's very small, but I'm sure I shall love him, and I mean to take care of him when he is older."

Mrs. Ainsworth had dreaded the ordeal of the first meeting. She feared Philip might show some jealousy, but the sweet manner of the boy quite satisfied her and made her very happy.

When Bassett spoke of Philip's nose being out of joint, the boy laughed, and rubbing his finger over that small feature declared that it was as straight as ever. "I guess there's room enough for both of us in this big house, and it'll be jolly by and by, when he can run about and play with Père Josef's 'children.' I'll bet *he* won't scream when he sees them."

Madam Ainsworth was as fussily fond of the new-comer as she was of Lucille. It had been a great sorrow to her that there was no one of the blood to inherit the name as well as the money. She could not bear to think that the little waif would be the only Ainsworth in the future; that a boy she could never love would be her only grandson. This child had come to make her last days happy and peaceful, and a little prince was never received with greater rejoicing than was the tiny pink being who, watched with loving care, lay sleeping in his lace-trimmed cradle.

Philip heard and saw all these demonstrations of satisfaction unmoved. It is true his blue eyes grew deeper and more serious, while his face thinned and paled daily. When the autumn winds blew rough and piercing he complained of the cold, and Bassett noticed that he had a harsh little cough, but nobody else noticed it. The old butler gave him hoarhound drops, but Philip handed them over to the first small beggar he met, while he drew his thick little ulster closer around him, glad that winter had come, for *this* winter they would surely take him home. Mrs. Ainsworth's lungs were delicate, and already they were talking of going south toward spring. "It must be soon now," Philip said to himself, as he counted away the weeks, hoping and waiting cheerfully.

CHAPTER XXIV

A JOYFUL MEETING

ONE day in January, Madam Ainsworth came down-stairs wrapped in furs from head to foot. She was going out for an airing, and as she stepped into the hall she was surprised to see Philip sitting before the open fire. He had drawn a large leather-covered chair close to the fender, while he leaned back against the cushion with closed eyes and folded hands. There was something touching in the boy's languid position and pale, tired face. Madam Ainsworth thought him sleeping, but when he heard her step, he started to his feet, a little confused and flushed.

"Why, Philip," she said kindly, "are you cold that you get so near the fire?"

"I was a little cold—not very," he replied, trying to smile brightly.

"Have you been out to-day?" she asked, looking at him closely; for the first time she noticed how thin he was.

"No, Madam; I haven't been out. I had no lessons to-day, but I'm going for a walk by and by."

"Wouldn't you rather go for a drive? Get your fur coat and cap, and come with me."

It was not the first time during the winter that Madam Ainsworth had invited Philip to drive with her. Since Mrs. Van Norcom went away she had no one to drive with her every day, and rather than go alone she sometimes took Philip. Mrs. Van Norcom had decided that her health was much better abroad, and, in consideration of that she concluded to make Paris her permanent home; therefore she, Lucille, the poodle, the governess, and Helen had left New York soon after the arrival of Mrs. Ainsworth's little boy. Madam Ainsworth would have accompanied them had it not been for her interest in her little grandson, who, after all, was of greater importance than the little heiress.

When she invited Philip to go out with her, the boy went rather indifferently for his coat. He did not much care for this ceremonious drive.

The park was very dreary now: the trees were leafless, there was not a vestige of green, and in all the shady places were little patches of snow. The ponds were frozen over, and his birds were gone. They had flown away south, where he longed to follow them.

As they drove up the avenue near to the entrance of the park, Philip's attention was attracted by a group of boys gathered around a forlorn, ragged little negro. The black mite's back was turned toward Philip, his fists were crammed into his eyes, and he was boo-hooing loudly. There had been a fight, and evidently the little ragamuffin had had the worst of it. Philip was interested instantly, and turned to stare at the group. Suddenly he started to his feet and almost shouted:

"It is—it *is* Lilybel! Thomas," he cried, seizing the colored coachman by the arm, "stop, and let me get out! It's Lilybel, and those boys are ill-treating him. Stop, and let me go, quick!"

Thomas drew up his horses shortly at the imperative command, and without a word to Madam Ainsworth, Philip sprang out of the carriage, and rushed into the group of boys.

The old lady did not know what had happened until, almost overcome with surprise and mortification, she saw the boy push through the throng, who scattered right and left, and clasp—yes, actually clasp—the hands of the worst-looking specimen of colored humanity that she had ever seen.

Thomas, with a knowing grin, turned, and, touching his hat, looked at his mistress interrogatively.

"Yes," she said, faintly, "go on quickly; the boy must be insane."

When the group of rough-looking gamins saw the handsome, well-dressed boy spring from the fine carriage and hurry toward them, they scattered instantly, and left Philip and Lilybel the center of a crowd of curious spectators.

At first the little negro did not recognize Philip, who almost deluged him with a stream of questions. "Where did you come from? How did you get here? When did you come? Is Seline with you?" and the like, to which Lilybel replied, still whimpering and rubbing his eyes:

"Is 't you, Mars' Philip? My, my! I didn't know 't war you—an' a coat on like a b'ar! I 's done been a-huntin' ev'rywhar fer yer; an' what good clo'es yer got!" And Lilybel looked at his old friend admiringly, while he shivered as much from his joy and excitement as from the cold.

"How did you get here?" repeated Philip, excitedly. "Tell me how you came here."

"I done cum in one o' dem big steamboats. My ma she gwine ter whip me good 'ca'se—'ca'se I los' her money. I jes' tuk it ter go ter er cirkus an' buy some ging'-pop, an' my ma she war awful mad; she say she war gwine ter whip me till I couldn't stan', so I jes' run erway an' hid on one of dem bustin' big steamboats; an' I was sick—I was awful sick." And Lilybel sniffed again at the thought of the miseries of his voluntary sea-voyage.

"Oh, Lilybel, you did wrong to run away," said Philip, reprovingly. "What will poor Seline do?"

"PHILIP RUSHED INTO THE GROUP OF BOYS."

"My ma? I s'pects she's glad 'ca'se I 's dade; she thinks I 's dade, 'ca'se I frowed my jacket an' hat inter der ruver, so she'd think I 's drownded."

113

"Why, Lilybel, how wicked! I'm sorry you were so wicked," cried Philip, greatly shocked at the depravity of his friend. "But when was that? How long ago? Tell me all about it."

"Oh, it war las' fall. I 's be'n yere more 'n a year, an' I 's be'n lookin' fer yer all der time."

"Where have you been living ever since?" questioned Philip.

"Over dar," pointing toward the east side, "with a colored lady what keeps a boardin'-house; an' she's awful mean. She whip me good 'ca'se I pick up some money on der floor an' didn't guv it ter her. I foun' it, I did; an' it war mine. She whip me, an' war er-gwine ter send fer a bobby, so I run erway, an' I 's be'n er-lookin' fer yer, Mars' Philip."

"Dear me! what a hard time you've had, Lilybel," said Philip, sympathetically; "but the money wasn't yours because you found it."

"Yes, it war, Mars' Philip. I *foun'* it; I didn't stole it."

Philip felt that it was useless to try to make Lilybel understand the difference between *meum* and *tuum;* so, looking pityingly at his fluttering rags and broken shoes, he said:

"Well, come home with me. I'll ask my mama to give you some clothes. Don't cry any more; I'll take care of you. Come on with me."

And Philip, hailing a passing car, ushered Lilybel into it, and got in himself, as proudly as though his companion were dressed in purple and fine linen.

An hour after, Philip, all energy and animation, rushed into Mrs. Ainsworth's room without even the ceremony of knocking.

"Oh, Mama," he cried, joyfully, "Lilybel is here!"

"Who is Lilybel?" asked Mrs. Ainsworth, surprised and puzzled. She had quite forgotten the name of the droll little darky who had brought the basket when Philip came to stay with them.

"Why, Mama, don't you remember Seline's Lilybel?" demanded Philip, in a hurt voice.

"Oh, yes, I remember now; the little colored boy in New Orleans."

"Yes, that's the one; he's here, and he hasn't any clothes; he's ragged and cold. I found him in the street; he ran away and came here on a steamer, and he's been looking for me. Some boys were fighting him because he hadn't any one to take his part; they hit him after he was down. Don't you call it mean to hit a fellow after he's down? But when they saw me they ran away like cowards. If they hadn't, I would have paid them off."

"Oh, Philip! *would* you engage in a street fight?" asked Mrs. Ainsworth, with some disgust in her voice.

"Yes, Mama, I would, if I saw any boy, especially Lilybel, imposed upon. But say, Mama, may I give Lilybel some of my clothes—I've got so many; and may I ask Mr. Butler to give him some dinner; and can he stay here?"

"Stay here, Philip; why, that is impossible! We have nowhere to put him, and even if we had, we would have to get Madam Ainsworth's permission first."

"But he can go in the stable with Thomas. If I ask Thomas he will take care of him."

Mrs. Ainsworth looked distressed. "Really, my dear, I don't know what to say until I ask your papa. You can give the boy the brown suit you wore last winter, and you may ask Bassett for some food for him, but as to his staying here, I can't give you an answer now. However, you can take him to the stable for the present."

Philip went off joyfully to search his wardrobe, and before another hour, Lilybel was transformed into a respectable-looking boy; and Thomas had consented to allow him to share his quarters, if Madam Ainsworth made no objections.

That evening there was a sound of revelry in the stable. Philip disappeared directly after dinner, and Bassett was seen to slip out the back way with something in a basket covered with a napkin. Lilybel was in clover, and Philip was happier than he had been for a long time.

CHAPTER XXV

A Crisis

MADAM AINSWORTH did not consent, neither did she positively refuse to allow Lilybel to become an inmate of the stable. She simply regarded the matter as something beneath her consideration. For some time everything went on peacefully, and Philip was delighted with the excellent conduct of his friend. The only objectionable feature in the arrangement was that, in spite of Mr. and Mrs. Ainsworth's orders to the contrary, Philip spent most of his time in the stable with his funny little protégé and the friendly Thomas, whose society was not exactly conducive to refinement and good morals; but there was a fascination about the small rascal that Philip could not resist. He did not intend to be disobedient, but almost before he was aware of it, he was sitting on a box in the feed room, chatting about his old home, Dea, and Seline.

Mrs. Ainsworth, happy and satisfied in her new motherhood, did not see that the boy was starving for affection, and that his distaste for his books, and even his drawing, his lassitude and indifference, were the result of failing health. She noticed how thin and pale he was, but she thought he was growing too fast, that his condition was due to the transition period which she had spoken of. And she was right in one way. It was due to transition—a transition from affection and interest to neglect and indifference, from his soft, sunny South to the cold, austere North, from a simple, natural life to one of hothouse culture and ultra-civilization. He was a transplanted wild flower, and the experiment had not worked well; he did not thrive in the rich parterre of his new garden.

One day Philip asked Lilybel if he would like to go home. The little negro grinned and said: "Yas, Mars' Philip." Then he added, very decidedly: "But I ain't er-gwine ter go t' New 'leens in no steamboat; I 's er-gwine ter *walk*."

"Oh, but it's too far to walk," returned Philip. "I guess it would take more than a week to walk there." He had a very vague idea of the distance.

"I could git lots o' lifts on dem freight-trains," returned Lilybel, eagerly; "but I 's 'feared ter go alone. Mars' Philip, why don't yer run erway an' go too?"

"Oh, I wouldn't run away. I want to go *awful*, but I wouldn't run away. Besides, there's no need of it; my papa and mama are going to take me soon, and you can go with us. I guess Seline will be glad to see you."

Lilybel hung his head and grinned an affirmative, although he was not quite sure that his "ma" would receive him with rapture.

Shortly after this conversation, and about the time when Philip thought his long-cherished hopes were near to being realized, Mr. Ainsworth was suddenly called away on very urgent business in the far West, connected with a railroad in which not only Madam Ainsworth, but also the little heiress, had large interests; and again Philip saw the vision of his old home fade away into an indefinite future.

About this time Lilybel struck up a sudden intimacy with a boot-black older than himself and of doubtful character, and he would have introduced his new chum into the select society of the stable had Thomas allowed him to do so. However, Lilybel spent a great deal of time with him, and would remain away for days together. When he returned he would be half clothed, dirty, and hungry. This was a severe tax on Philip's wardrobe as well as on his patience; but this was not the worst. Often, after these sudden departures, some little thing would be missed by the servants—a spoon or fork by Bassett, a little money by the cook, or some of the kitchen-maid's jewelry.

Gradually Lilybel had worked his way into the house—into the kitchen, the pantry, up the back stairs to Philip's room; and one day when Madam Ainsworth found him gravely examining the articles on her toilet-table, she said she could endure no more. The visit to her room accounted for the disappearance, some time before, of a valuable ring. The boy was a thief, and he must go, or she would send for an officer to arrest him.

Philip was in a dreadful state of terror; the thought of Lilybel being sent to prison was unendurable. He could not believe his protégé was guilty, but he took him aside and lectured him severely, gave him a fresh supply of clothes, and some of his pocket-money, and bade him go out and find a place where he could earn his bread and meat.

Lilybel promised humbly to do as Philip told him, but in a week he was back, hanging around the stable in a most forlorn condition. When Philip was secretly called out to him, the little rascal was sniffling and shivering with cold. His warm jacket was gone, and he had got rid of his shoes. It was freezing, and the little beggar's bare feet made Philip's heart ache; he was in despair, not knowing what to do with his troublesome dependent. There was only one thing that he could think of, and that was to beg the soft-hearted Thomas to smuggle him into the stable again, until he could find some way out of the dilemma.

"I's mos' starved, I is," was Lilybel's first complaint, when he was once more installed in the comfortable stable.

"Oh, Lilybel, what *did* you do with the money I gave you?" said Philip, in a discouraged voice. "Why didn't you get something to eat?"

"I is, Mars' Philip. I 's got can' peaches an' sardines."

"But why didn't you get bread and meat?"

"'Ca'se I likes can' peaches an' sardines der bes'."

What could Philip say to such reasoning? Again Bassett was taken into the boy's confidence, and again the kind old soul stood by his little friend, and secretly, and with many misgivings, furnished food for the hungry Lilybel.

In the house nothing more was heard of Philip's troublesome protégé, and Madam Ainsworth congratulated herself that she had got rid of a nuisance, when one day, as she approached the entrance to her house, she was surprised to see a crowd of men and boys around her steps. Her first thought was of fire within; but no, their attention seemed to be centered on something without. When Thomas drew up hurriedly before the door, and she made her way through the tightly packed throng, she saw with horror a sign on the upper step. It was made of the top of a pasteboard box, and on it was rudely printed with shoe-blacking, "*Wite Mise ter sea five sents a site.*" Beside the sign was Lilybel, in one of Philip's best jackets, and near him sat the shoeblack holding the cage that contained Père Josef's children, while he set forth, in a loud voice, the many accomplishments of the tiny creatures, who, frightened by the strange crowd, raced and scampered about the cage with astonishing rapidity.

Madam Ainsworth almost fainted. "Thomas, disperse the crowd," she gasped, as she made her way up the steps. "And take these away," indicating the cage, the sign, and Lilybel.

To the credit of Philip we will say that he was with his tutor, and knew nothing about the exhibition. It was entirely a business arrangement between Lilybel and the shoeblack.

LILYBEL GIVES AN EXHIBITION.

When Madam Ainsworth ferreted out the truth, that Lilybel was again installed in the stable, and that Philip was aware of it, her indignation knew no bounds, and for a moment she came near turning her son's adopted son and the "children" out of the house forever.

Again, as he had done a year before, Philip was obliged to plead for the innocent "children," but this time with less pleasant results. The crisis had come, and there was no temporizing. Lilybel at least must go, and go permanently; as to the fate of the poor "children," Philip was for a time left in a state of harrowing uncertainty.

CHAPTER XXVI

"Good Night, Mr. Butler"

A FEW days after the exhibition on the front steps, Madam Ainsworth was sitting in her drawing-room talking very earnestly with her old friend, and her voice was raised somewhat above its usual well-bred level.

"If they had consulted *me* it never would have happened," she said, decidedly. "They were too hasty, and now they regret it."

"Naturally, they would like their own son to be the elder," the friend placidly answered.

"Certainly, they would; but it's not only that. They are tired of the boy; he hasn't turned out as they expected. As he grows older, very common traits develop in his character. And what else can you expect from a child brought up by an old colored woman? Lately he has had a little negro thief here to whom he is devoted. We have had a terrible struggle to keep the little rascal away from the premises; and even now I dare say Philip meets him outside."

"How fortunate the little heiress isn't here this winter," remarked the friend.

"Oh, if Lucille hadn't gone abroad with her mother, I should have insisted on his being sent away. The poor child suffered enough through him last winter," said Madam Ainsworth, angrily. "And now Edward and Laura are as miserable as they can be, and all on account of that troublesome boy. They don't love him now as they thought they did. I'll give them the credit of *thinking* they were fond of him, but they never really loved the boy; and now that they have one of their own, they *know* it."

"It's a very unfortunate situation, is it not?" said the friend. "They can't very well get rid of him, can they?"

"No, that's just it; they can't. I should not be sorry if he should take it into his head to run off with some of his low companions where they could never hear from him again."

"Dear me, and to think of all they have done for him! It would be a terrible change for the boy after his life of luxury," said the friend, smoothly.

"Oh, I think he would prefer a gipsy life. There's no doubt in my mind of his being the child of very common parents; and to think that Edward should adopt him without knowing!"

"It's going to be very bad for their own son to have such a boy for an elder brother—for you know children are so imitative."

"Yes, it's dreadful any way you look at it," returned Madam Ainsworth, with a heavy sigh. "And just now, when I could be so happy with my grandson, to have it all spoiled by that little waif—that little intruder into my family! And as far as I can see, there's no way to get rid of him."

When Madam Ainsworth and her friend left the drawing-room, after some more confidential chatter, there was a slight movement behind the curtain that draped the alcove of the window, and Philip slipped out silently and timidly. He was very pale, and his eyes had a wild, frightened look. He had been sitting there watching the people in the street when the old ladies entered, and he had unwillingly heard every word of their conversation.

Later in the day, when Madam Ainsworth was returning from a visit of charity, as her carriage crossed Seventh Avenue she saw Philip and Lilybel standing on a corner talking together very earnestly. "It's just as I thought," she said to herself; "he sees that little ragamuffin outside. What in the world can he wish to say to him? I really dread the result of having that boy under our roof!"

When Philip entered the drawing-room just before dinner, they all noticed how excited he appeared, and how carelessly he was dressed.

"That boy is not fit to come into the drawing-room," said Madam Ainsworth in a low, vexed voice to her daughter-in-law. "He is so untidy, and utterly indifferent to his dress!"

"I'm very sorry," returned Mrs. Ainsworth, flushing a little. "Perhaps it's my fault. I'm afraid I have neglected him lately; he certainly has changed in appearance."

Philip noticed Madam Ainsworth's look of disgust, and heard her unkind words; for his senses were very acute, and his heart very sore. He was looking at a book, and he bent his head lower over it to hide the tears that sprang to his eyes. When dinner was announced, he walked out silently behind the others, and took his accustomed place without a word.

Bassett was distressed because the boy ate nothing; and when the dessert came out he slipped a generous plate of macaroons and bonbons into a drawer, saying to himself, "The little chap shall 'ave these to-night. 'E 's hill and un'appy. I'm going to cheer 'im hup with these."

"BASSETT GAVE HIM A HEARTY CLASP."

While Bassett was putting away the silver, Philip slipped softly into the pantry, and stood near the old man, watching him wistfully. He wanted to say something, but his heart was too full. When Bassett took out the bonbons and gave them to him, he could not control himself; his lips quivered pitifully, and large tears rolled over his face.

"Why—why, Master Philip, my little man, what's the matter? What's 'appened?" cried Bassett, astonished at such signs of trouble in his usually merry little friend.

"Oh, nothing, Mr. Butler; but—but you're so good to me, and it makes me cry *now* when—when any one is good to me."

"Yes, I see, my poor little lad. You hain't has rugged has you used to be; I see you're losing your happetite, an' that won't do. You mustn't fret. It's halong of that new boy; they're all so taken hup with 'im that they don't think of no one else."

"Oh, I don't mind that, Mr. Butler. Well," with a heavy sigh and a fresh burst of tears, "I'm—I'm going to my room now. Good night, Mr. Butler; good night." Still he lingered, with his hand on the door. Suddenly he turned to Bassett and said, almost entreatingly, "I wish—I wish—you'd shake hands with me, Mr. Butler."

"Why, bless your 'eart, my dear little lad, hof course I will." And Bassett gave him such a hearty clasp that Philip smiled through his tears.

"And—and you won't—you won't forget me, will you?"

"Forget you? Why, 'ow you do talk! 'Ow am I a-going to forget you when I see you every day?"

"But when I'm not here; when—when I go away you'll stand up for me? You'll say I wasn't a bad boy, won't you?"

"That I will, Master Philip. I'll stand hup for you has long has I've a leg to stand on."

"Oh, thank you! Good night, and thank you for the candy and cake." And with a look eloquent of mingled sorrow and affection, Philip hurried out.

When he had gone, Bassett stood for some time looking thoughtfully at the forks in his hand; then he muttered to himself: "Hit's too bad the way they slight that pretty, kind-'earted little chap; hand what's 'e got in his 'ead to-night? 'E's that blue 'e halmost made me cry myself. I must try to cheer 'im hup to-morrow."

When Philip reached his room, he looked around him nervously; then he opened the door cautiously and listened. They were all below in the drawing-room. There were visitors; once in a while he heard the sound of laughter and conversation. They were all very much engaged; they were not thinking of him. After standing silent a moment in deep thought, he went to a drawer, and from the very bottom of it he drew out the red and yellow silk kerchief belonging to the "children." This, with a thick woolen one which he wore in cold weather to protect his throat, he wrapped carefully around the cage and tied securely. Then he took a small bag which Mrs. Ainsworth had given him for his school-books, and lifting from the upper shelf of his wardrobe a paper box, he removed from it the crumpled funeral wreath with the motto, *"À ma mère,"* enveloped in the piece of crape—Dea's last gift. These he carefully folded in paper and deposited in the bottom of the bag. On his table lay the little Bible and Prayer-book—Toinette's gift: these he also placed with the wreath. Then he opened his small safe, and taking out his savings which he had hoarded with great self-denial, he counted them over and over; there was not so much as he thought he had, but he had drawn heavily on them to supply Lilybel's exorbitant demands. However, he put what there was in his pocket-book, and that, with Bassett's paper of bonbons, he dropped into the bag with his other treasures. From his wardrobe he selected his oldest suit, his oldest shoes and cap; and when he had put them on he hesitated a moment over the fur coat. It was so warm—but no: it had cost a great deal; he would not take it. He hung it up, and instead of it he selected a plain little ulster. It was thick and warm, but not so warm as the rejected fur coat.

When he was dressed he opened the door and listened. There was no one on the back landing; he knew he could slip out that way without being seen, so he took the "children" in one hand, and the bag in the other. They were his own little belongings, and they were all he had; and silently and tremblingly he crept, like a little culprit, down the back stairs and out into the street.

It was early in March, and a wretched drizzling night, half rain and half snow. Philip shivered and coughed as he stepped upon the sidewalk. For a moment he hesitated; then with a last sorrowful look at the luxurious home he was leaving, he went out in the cold and darkness with only Père Josef's little "children" for company.

CHAPTER XXVII

THE EMPTY ROOM

THE next morning after Philip's departure, Madam Ainsworth and her daughter-in-law were sitting at the breakfast-table alone. Neither of the ladies ate much, and both seemed preoccupied and troubled. When the meal was nearly over, Mrs. Ainsworth looked up suddenly and said, as if it had just occurred to her, "Why, where is Philip this morning? He is always so punctual; I'm afraid he is ill."

"If you please, Madam," remarked Bassett, with a little tremor in his voice, "I will go to 'is room and hinquire."

"Yes, go," replied Madam Ainsworth, petulantly; "and tell him to come down immediately—that we have nearly finished breakfast. I hope the boy isn't going to be dilatory. It will be very trying if he is."

"He never has been," said Mrs. Ainsworth, excusingly; "he is always down before we are. I notice he coughs lately; I'm afraid he is not well. I must really consult the doctor; I confess I am worried about him."

"Oh, he has a little cold, I suppose," said Madam Ainsworth, indifferently; "but it's not his health I should worry about."

"Why, what has he done now?" asked Mrs. Ainsworth, surprised. "I hope there is no new trouble"; and before her mother-in-law could reply, Bassett entered hurriedly and unceremoniously.

"The room 's hempty!" he exclaimed; "and Master Philip's gone!"

The old man was pale, and trembled visibly. His strange manner alarmed Mrs. Ainsworth. "Gone!" she cried, starting up excitedly. "What do you mean? Gone where?"

"Oh, I don't know where 'e 's gone, poor little lad," replied Bassett, in a broken voice. "Hall I know his that 'is room his hempty, and that 'e didn't sleep in 'is bed last night; 'e must 'ave left last night."

"What! Has he been gone all night? Out alone in the dark and cold! Oh, what can have happened to him?" gasped Mrs. Ainsworth, pale and trembling. "He must have met with some dreadful accident to keep him away all night!"

"Hit was not han haccident, Madam," said the butler, gravely. "Hin my hopinion, Master Philip's gone with the hintention of staying, because 'e 'as taken 'is cage of little mice with 'im."

"Run away! Just what I expected he would do!" exclaimed Madam Ainsworth. She was so excited that she quite forgot Bassett was in the room.

"Please don't condemn him until you know," pleaded Mrs. Ainsworth. "I can't think he has gone of his own will; he loved us so, and was so—so grateful and happy."

"I beg your pardon, Madam," interposed Bassett, decidedly; "if I may be hallowed to say hit, Master Philip 'as n't been 'appy for some time. I don't know what was hin 'is little mind, but now I think of hit, I might 'ave known that something was a-going to 'appen by the way 'e came to me in the pantry last night, and hasked me to stand hup for 'im when he was gone"—

"Oh, you knew it, did you?" interrupted Madam Ainsworth, severely; "and you never told. Really, Bassett, you astonish me."

"No, I didn't *know* nothing, Madam," returned Bassett, firmly; "I honly thought the pretty little lad was hill hand down hin spirits, hand I tried to cheer 'im hup; then when 'e said good night, 'e—was a-cryin'."

"Did he say anything, Bassett? Did he tell you where he was going?" asked Mrs. Ainsworth, anxiously.

"Not a word, Madam; 'e didn't heven say that 'e was going; honly 'inted at something."

"Oh, I am to blame; it is my fault," cried Mrs. Ainsworth, regretfully. "Since I had Baby I have neglected the poor boy. I didn't mean to, but I have. I have driven him away. What shall I do? How shall I find him?" And Mrs. Ainsworth looked appealingly at her mother-in-law.

"My dear Laura, don't be foolish. It is absurd to make a fuss about that boy," said Madam Ainsworth, coldly. "The ungrateful little creature has grown tired of your kindness, and he has gone back to his former condition. In plain words, he has run away. I saw him again with that little negro only yesterday. They were plotting then; and if you remember, he seemed guilty last night. He was ashamed to look one in the face."

"I remember that he seemed excited and troubled, but I should not say that that was an indication of guilt. I can't understand it; I can't think he would go voluntarily, and without a word to me. I wish Edward were here. I don't know what to do; I don't know what steps to take!" cried Mrs. Ainsworth, despairingly.

"Bassett, did you notice whether he had taken his clothing?" asked Madam Ainsworth.

"I should say, Madam, that 'e 'ad honly took what 'e 'ad hon. I looked hin 'is wardrobe; hit was full, hand 'is little fur coat was there."

"Oh, well, then you can depend on his coming back. He has gone off on some expedition with those low companions of his. When he is tired and hungry he will return."

"But we ought to do something now," urged Mrs. Ainsworth, "I can't let the matter rest and wait for him to come back."

"I should advise you to do so," returned Madam Ainsworth, indifferently. "I suspect that the bootblack and the little negro have persuaded the boy to go off and exhibit those horrid little animals. One can't tell what absurd ideas they have put in his head. In any case, I should advise you to wait at least for a few days, and avoid all talk and excitement. It would be ridiculous to make a great fuss, and then have him come back, hungry and dirty, just as the little negro did. No doubt it is one of his pleasant little tricks to surprise and alarm us."

"I wish I could think so," said Mrs. Ainsworth, sadly. "I wish he would come back this moment, well and unharmed."

"And I wish he would stay away," thought Madam Ainsworth, as she left the breakfast-room. "I think we should be well rid of him."

Bassett went about with a very sorrowful face. Thinking of Philip's strange manner the preceding evening, he felt that the boy had said good-by instead of good night. "Pretty little lad, 'e was that un'appy that 'e couldn't bear hit hany longer," thought Bassett, as he worked and pondered; "so 'e just took them little hanimals and went hoff hall halone last night. Dear me, what's to become hof a delicate little chap like that?"

Several days passed. Philip did not return, and nothing was heard of him. The bootblack was questioned concerning Lilybel, but he could give no information. The little negro had vanished too; evidently he and Philip had gone together.

When Mrs. Ainsworth examined the boy's room, she was fully convinced that he did not intend to return. She missed the funeral wreath, the Bible, and prayer-book, and she knew that he had gone forever, and taken his treasures with him. In spite of Madam Ainsworth's advice, she was not satisfied to let the matter rest. After a week had passed and there was no news of the missing boy, she wrote to her husband for advice, and at the same time employed a detective to find Philip. She was conscience-stricken and dismayed when she fully realized how she had neglected the child and left him to himself. "It is my fault," she would think regretfully. "He has a beautiful nature; he was so affectionate, so generous. I could have made anything of him. He would have been good and happy if I had not seemed to forget him—if I had not neglected my duty. If he is lost, if he is ruined, I alone am to blame."

CHAPTER XXVIII

PÈRE JOSEF SENDS A PACKAGE OF LETTERS

WHEN Père Josef, after long and weary journeyings through the mountainous regions of New Mexico, returned at last to the little mission of San Miguel, he found a letter, written months before, from his friend Père Martin of St. Mary's, telling him of the death of Toinette, and of the adoption of Philip by the Northern artist and his wife. Whereupon, Père Josef wrote immediately to Père Martin, asking that a certain package of papers left in his care be forwarded as soon as possible to the Mission of San Miguel; but long before the papers reached him Père Josef was off on another journey, longer and more arduous than the preceding, and it was well on in the second winter of his mission when he returned to San Miguel and found the package awaiting him.

One night, alone in his little cell, weary, disheartened, and homesick, Père Josef broke the seal of a large brown envelop addressed to him in a feeble, almost illegible scrawl. Within it were several papers and quite a number of letters. The first one he opened and glanced at bore the signature of Toinette, and read as follows:

DEAR PÈRE JOSEF: The doctor says I have heart disease and may die suddenly; that is why I write this letter to you, and why I give you these papers to keep and to open only after I am at rest. I want to have everything plain and clear for my boy when I am gone, and when you read this letter you will understand all about it.

You may think that I ought to have told you all this long ago, but I never could. I never could decide to be parted from my boy, and I knew you would tell me that it was my duty to give him up.

I must begin at the beginning, and try to tell you all as plainly as I can. I was brought up by the Detrava family with great care and kindness. I was taught to speak French and English, to read, write, and embroider, and also to plant and cultivate flowers. When my young mistress, Miss Estelle, was born, I was thirty. They put the babe in my arms; she was mine from that hour, and I belonged to her. She grew up pretty and good. I watched over her, and loved her better than anything on earth. When the war came, and she lost both father and mother, she was more mine than ever. It was hard to live then; every one was for himself, and no one remembered the desolate orphan. I put my arms around her and held her up when she was ready to fall. She was life and everything to me.

There was an encampment of Union soldiers near our plantation. They were our enemies, but they did not molest us. The young captain in charge was very good to us. He pitied my young mistress, and did all he could to protect us and make us comfortable, and he was so gentle and kind that we could not help liking him and trusting him. You know what a feeling there was at that time, and how secretly everything had to be done. I saw how it all was, but I did not know how it would end for my poor child. Well, one night they were privately married by a strange French priest. He had come to our parish to take the place of our curé, who had gone as chaplain in a Confederate regiment. Père Josef, you were the priest who married them.

Here Père Josef looked up from the letter, and sat for some time in deep thought. "Yes," he said at length to himself, "I remember it. It was while I was in St. John the Baptist. It was one night in the little vestry, the poor young things came to me, and I couldn't refuse. Those were stirring times, and strange things happened. Yes, I remember; a pale, lovely girl and a young Union officer. I thought it very strange, but I married them. Yes, this is the certificate I gave them," and he unfolded a paper and saw his own signature. Then he went on reading Toinette's letter.

Now I have recalled that to you, you will remember what followed. A year after you baptized their child, a beautiful boy, and when the child was scarce two months old, the young father was killed in a skirmish, and my mistress, the child, and a nurse fled from the country to the city house, which, as you may remember, was burnt that very night. All three were supposed to have perished in the flames. It is true the young mother lost her life, but the child and nurse did not. I am the nurse, and Philip is the child. When the fire broke out, the babe was asleep in my arms. I carried him to a place of safety, and then went back to try to save my dear mistress; but I was too late. I could not find her. When I heard that the nurse and child were supposed to be buried in the ruins, I took the baby, without any one noticing me, and fled to a friend in another part of the city. She gave me shelter, and kept my secret until she died. After her death I went back to the Detrava place. I wanted the boy to grow up on his own property; he didn't know that it was his, but I knew that it would some day belong to him.

PÈRE JOSEF READS TOINETTE'S LETTER.

Do you remember when I first brought Philip to you, how closely and severely you questioned me about his parentage? You did not remember me, and you did not dream that the boy was the child of Estelle Detrava and the young Union officer.

You will wonder why I concealed the truth and kept my secret so long. I will tell you: I loved the child; he was the only one left of his family, and it seemed as though he belonged to me, and that it would kill me to lose him; but the strongest reason of all was, I had solemnly promised my young mistress that if she should be taken away, I would never part with the child. For a reason very natural then she was set against his being brought up in the North. She knew that her husband had never made his marriage known to his family, because of the bitter feeling between the two parts of the country. She was proud and sensitive about it, and she made me promise over and over that if she and her young husband died, I would keep the boy, at least until he was old enough to choose for himself. I was afraid if I gave him up that he would be sent North to his father's family, and that I should be parted from him. They knew nothing about him, and perhaps they would not care for him, and he was my very life. No, I couldn't give him up then, but I thought I could when he got older. That time—the time to give him up—has never come, and I think and hope it never will until I am where I cannot miss him, or fret to lose him.

But I must finish this, because writing tires me and is slow work. I have been days and nights over this confession, trying to make it all clear and plain. After the excitement about the fire was over, I went secretly back to the deserted plantation-house and got all of my young mistress's papers, which fortunately she left behind her in her hurried flight, or they would have been lost with her. I knew they would be needed some day. They are all in this package—the certificates which you gave, and a number of letters from the young officer to my mistress; and you will see that there is a letter addressed to the young man's mother, which has never been opened. He gave it to my mistress, so that if anything happened to him she could send it to his mother. I suppose that in it he confesses his marriage and asks them to take care of his wife and child. But she, blessed saint, will never need their care. She went to heaven, as her young husband had a few days before her; and now there is none left but the boy, who, when I am gone, must be given to his father's family. It may be wrong to keep him from them now, but he is only a little fellow and he loves me dearly. I have done my best for him: I have taught him to be good. No one can say a word against Toinette's Philip; and oh, Père Josef, I just feel that when you read this he will be alone! I shall be gone—the "mammy" he has always loved and obeyed. Will you do your best for the child, love him, comfort him—he will be so unhappy away from me? Of course these letters and papers must be sent to his grandmother. I wonder if she will love him as I have! Oh, Père Josef, be good to him! I leave him in your care; and if I have done wrong by keeping him, forgive me, and commend me to the mercy of God.

TOINETTE.

When Père Josef finished Toinette's letter, he furtively wiped a tear from his thin cheek; then, after looking over the papers carefully, he inclosed all, with a few explanatory lines from himself, in a strong package, which he addressed to Madam Ainsworth, "No.—Madison Avenue, New York."

133

CHAPTER XXIX

THE LITTLE PILGRIMS

IT is not our intention to follow in detail the wanderings and adventures of Philip and Lilybel. Their experiences on their pilgrimage toward the city of their destination would fill too many pages for our purpose.

When Philip went forth on that dreary March night, with Père Josef's "children" and his little bag of treasures, he had formed no plans as to the beginning or continuation of his journey. His first idea was to get away, his second was to get to New Orleans. The first did not seem so difficult, and was soon put into execution; but the latter required some serious consideration, as all roads do not lead to that fair and far city of the South.

In some respects a pedestrian journey has its advantages. One has no difficulty in choosing between sea and land, or deciding between rival lines of steamers and railroads; but it is very important that one should at least set out on the highway that leads to his destination.

Lilybel had been waiting some time at the corner. He was sniffling with cold and impatience; *he* also carried a bundle, but his bundle did not contain sentimental souvenirs of the past. Philip had not neglected the subsistence department of the expedition; he had given Lilybel money with which to buy provisions, and these provisions were tied up in the bundle, and consisted of bananas, gingerbread, and popped corn; a small tin bucket filled with molasses completed the outfit.

"Well," said Philip, curtly, on seeing him, "are you ready?"

"Yas, Mars' Philip, I 's ready, I 's got ev'ryt'ing; but be wes er-goin' ter stay out all night in der rain an' col'?"

"Yes, we are," returned Philip decidedly; "and we've got to *walk* to keep warm. Come on, let's start for the ferry." And without further parley he turned his face toward the river and trotted briskly along, followed by Lilybel, who lagged and sniffed and complained of the cold, pitifully.

As soon as Philip had started, he understood that he would be obliged to lead the expedition as well as to supply the moral force; therefore he debated in his mind just what was best to be done. The first thing was to get away from the city—"Or the bobbies 'll be arter us," Lilybel said, between his sniffs, "an' we'll be cotched an' sont back, an' dey 'll put us in der p'lice-station fer runnin' erway, an' wes 'll never git out."

This possibility really alarmed Philip. In spite of the dreadful unknown before him, he did not wish to be sent back, so he pressed on sturdily toward the ferry. He was neither cold nor wet; his thick little coat shed the rain, and his heart was warm with hope.

When they reached the ferry-slip, and Lilybel saw the boat and the dark waters of the North River, he hung back, saying stubbornly: "I ain't er-gwine on any steamboat ter New 'leens—I's er-gwine ter *walk*, I is."

"But you must cross the ferry first; this is only a ferry. Come on; the boat is about starting. If you don't come I'll go without you," returned Philip decidedly.

"I don't wanter," sniffled Lilybel, as Philip gave his tickets to the gate-keeper, and at the same time with an energetic push thrust the reluctant little darky into the thickest of the crowd, and so passed on unnoticed in the darkness. When they were once safely on the other side Philip walked a little slower; he was formulating a plan in his mind. With an intelligence beyond his years, he felt that it would not be well at first to make such inquiries as would cause any one to suspect his destination. If he was not very discreet he might furnish a clue that would lead to his being overtaken and sent back. Therefore he determined not to ask for directions which would awaken suspicion. He remembered distinctly two places which he had passed through on his way North with his adoptive parents. One was Chattanooga. It was impressed on his mind because they remained there in order to visit Lookout Mountain, the scene of the "battle in the clouds." The other was Washington; Mrs. Ainsworth had told him that it was the capital of the country. If they passed through those cities to come to New York, they could go South by the same route. So he decided to begin by inquiring the way to Washington.

So full of determination, so brave and hopeful was the boy, that he would not have been daunted or discouraged had he known of the long, weary days, weeks, and even months when he must always be moving on, of the cold, hunger, pain, and suffering he must endure, the hills, valleys, and forests, the rivers and lakes he must cross, before he could reach his desired haven.

When the night was half spent, the two little pilgrims found themselves beyond the blare and glare of Jersey City in a quiet sleeping suburb. Lilybel was exhausted, and declared he could go no farther; so they sat down on the steps of a half-finished house and munched a piece of the black gingerbread and a banana, after which Lilybel crawled under the steps among a pile of shavings, and was soon in the land of dreams, where one is seldom tired, cold, and hungry.

"LILYBEL RUBBED HIS EYES AND YAWNED, WHILE PHILIP SHOOK HIM VIGOROUSLY."

For some time Philip sat in the silence and looked at the stars. "There's the Dipper," he said to himself; "Mammy used to show it to me. It's just as bright here, and just as near, so it can't be far to New Orleans; and there's the Little Bear—it used to be right over the Pittosporum-tree in Mammy's garden. It looks just the same as it did then, and it's shining there and here at the same time." Sitting alone in the dark, with Père Josef's "children" hugged close to him, he felt that he had seen old friends in the Dipper and the Little Bear; that he would have their company on his long journey back to his home. He thought the way could not seem so long and dreary when they were shining above him. After awhile he felt cold and his eyes grew heavy with sleep. So he crawled under the steps beside Lilybel, who was in a comfortable nest of shavings, and placing the "children" between them, and his treasures under his head, he contentedly followed his little companion into the enchanting land of dreams.

At the earliest peep of day Philip was awakened by the scampering of the "children" in the cage. They were up early, and were indulging in a game of *Colin-Maillard*. Lilybel was still sleeping, and was safe to sleep all day if he was not disturbed.

"Why, Mars' Philip, it ain't time to git up!" he cried, dolorously, rubbing his eyes and yawning, while Philip shook him vigorously.

"Yes, it is; now hurry and eat your breakfast, and we'll start right off before any one is about."

Philip gave the "children" a few grains of popped corn, and ate a banana with a very poor appetite, while Lilybel fared sumptuously on a huge piece of gingerbread; then after making their toilet, which consisted in brushing off the clinging shavings and sawdust, they went on their way—but not rejoicing.

The morning was cold and gray. Philip's head ached and his feet felt like lead, but still he must press on, he must not give up when he had just begun the journey. Later, they stopped at a farm-house to ask for some water. It was breakfast-time, and the kind-hearted mother of a little boy gave them each a hot buttered roll and a cup of steaming coffee. This good fare cheered and encouraged them considerably, and they pressed on in quite a cheerful mood.

All day they walked, Philip resolutely, Lilybel laggingly. When they inquired the way to Washington, some laughed and some said: "Keep straight ahead and you'll get there in a week or so." Others told them they didn't know the way, that it was too far to walk there, and that they had better go by rail, and so on. Philip thanked them all with a gentle smile and trotted on serenely; but the day seemed the longest day that he had ever spent.

When night came on, they were near a railroad-station on the outskirts of a small village. Philip was very hungry, for he had eaten nothing since morning; but Lilybel had supplied himself by lightening his bundle to such an extent that nothing remained but a handful of popped corn, and for this dry fare Philip had no appetite. When they reached the station, a freight-train was pulled up on the track, and it seemed to be waiting for the engine in order to start. Two men were in the caboose, and as Philip was about to pass, he looked wistfully at them. They were eating supper, and had a pot of coffee between them. The tired boy craved some of the grateful beverage, but he did not like to beg, so he drew out a dime and asked them very politely if they would sell him some.

The men laughed heartily. "Why, my little man, we don't keep a coffee-stand; but I guess we can give you some." So they poured out a large tin cup full. It was strong and sweet, but it was not Mocha; yet Philip thought he had never tasted better. He gratefully drank half, and gave the remainder to Lilybel.

The little negro had been regarding the bread and bacon with an eloquent look, which the kind-hearted men appreciated. After the coffee disappeared, each little pilgrim received a generous plate of food, which they devoured eagerly. "Hunger is the best sauce." Philip relished his supper as he never did a meal served on Madam Ainsworth's dainty china by the capable and stately Bassett.

After they had eaten, Philip thanked the men politely, and was about to move on.

"Where are you goin', little fellows?" asked one, rough-looking without, but pure gold within.

"We're going to Washington," replied Philip, readily.

"Holy Moses! Ye are? How yer goin'?"

"We're going to walk," said Philip, undaunted.

"When do ye expect to git there?"

"Oh, I don't know; to-morrow, perhaps."

"Ha, ha! Well, git in here an' come along with us, and ye will; but if ye walk, it'll take a month, an' yer shoes 'll be all wore out."

Philip and Lilybel scrambled into the caboose with alacrity and delight. The kind occupants gave them a little bunk in the corner, where they slept comfortably; and in the morning they were in Washington, much to their satisfaction.

Philip would have liked to show the kind men the "children," but he was afraid to do so; he was wise enough to know that they would be another means of tracing him. So he could only thank his hospitable hosts very warmly as he walked away with a light heart.

"See here, Lilybel," he said confidently to his companion, "now we're a good long way from New York, we needn't be in such a hurry. I've got some money, and we'll stay here and rest awhile."

"An' yer can make lots more a-showin' dem little mices," suggested Lilybel, with a delighted grin. "Didn't I tole yer wes 'd git lots er lifts on dem trains? I guess now we won't have ter walk no more."

Philip was very hopeful; he quite agreed with Lilybel—everything was going so well. It would be very easy to get home, after all; so they sallied forth to see the city with the confidence and carelessness of a couple of young millionaires out for a holiday.

CHAPTER XXX

MADAM AINSWORTH RECEIVES A PACKAGE OF LETTERS

PHILIP had been gone a month. Mrs. Ainsworth had been very anxious and unhappy, and had certainly done all that she could in the absence of her husband and in the face of her mother-in-law's constant discouragement. A great many letters had passed between the detective employed and Mr. Ainsworth; the latter, remembering Lilybel's former methods of traveling, thought that the little negro, who had also disappeared, had induced Philip to hide with him on an outward-bound steamer, and that they were doubtless in New Orleans; but communications with the captains of the different steamers and the police of that city convinced them that the children had not gone by sea, nor had they, as far as he and the detective could learn, returned to their former home.

Madam Ainsworth, who was not at all anxious to have them discovered, was of the opinion that they had never left New York, and she was in daily fear that they would unexpectedly turn up, and that Philip would be forgiven and taken back. However, as weeks passed away she began to feel easier, and was more than vexed at her daughter-in-law for being anxious and worried about what she termed "unexpected good fortune." They had got rid of the little waif through no fault of theirs; they had not turned him off. He had gone of his own free will, and they were not in any way responsible for it. She did not see why they should search for him and want him back. If they succeeded in finding him, he would probably run away again, and they would have a repetition of all the trouble and expense. There was no doubt that the boy was something of a vagabond, and as he grew older he would be more unruly and troublesome; therefore they were well rid of him before he should disgrace them.

These were the specious arguments which she used with her daughter-in-law, and with which she quieted her own conscience; for now and then, in spite of her coldness and indifference, she had little twinges which made her very uncomfortable. Suddenly the boy's handsome face would come before her; she would think of his merry laugh, his gentle, kindly ways, and even his little mischievous tricks now made her smile and sigh at the same time. She remembered the day when he pleaded so earnestly for Père Josef's "children," and the touching tone in his voice that had moved her so, and brought back the pain of an old sorrow. And toward the last, just before he went away, he looked ill; sometimes she had noticed a flush on his cheeks, and an unnatural brightness in his eyes. Perhaps exposure and want had killed him, and even now his little neglected body might be lying in some unknown grave. These memories and fancies increased day by day. In spite of her satisfaction at his continued absence, the boy interested her, and occupied her thoughts away more than he had when he was with her.

One morning, when she sat down to her writing-table to open her letters, she saw on the top of the pile a large, strange-looking package addressed to her in an unknown hand.

Her fingers trembled a little as she broke the strong seal, and the first object within the cover that met her eye was a letter that bore her name in writing that she remembered too well—the writing of her son, her Philip, who for ten long years had sent her no missive to break the solemn silence between them. It was like a voice from the grave. With an awed face she opened it, and read the confession of his marriage, the tender passionate appeal to his mother for his wife and child.

Why had this been kept from her for all these years? Who had dared to do it? And a feeling of resentment was mingled with her sorrow and surprise. One after another she unfolded and read the papers: her son's tender little notes to the girl he loved, Père Josef's explanatory letter, and, last of all, Toinette's touching confession.

There it all lay before her, the history of these young lives: the joys, the sorrows, the hopes and ambitions, ending in a mournful tragedy, which seemed unreal and almost impossible because of its remoteness. Unknown to her, her son was married a year or more before his death. The swift memory of that awful day when she was told that he had fallen wrung her heart with pain. He had been taken away in the flush of youth and love, and his young wife had followed him; but the child,—where was the child? They spoke of

Philip's child, her grandson, the eldest Ainsworth. Why had they kept him from her all these years? Who had done it? Where was he?—and why were these letters sent to her now?

Her mind was in a state of terrible confusion. Again she read Toinette's letter, again Père Josef's, slowly and more carefully. Suddenly, and with awful force, the truth burst upon her. Toinette's Philip—that boy her son had adopted—the little waif, the vagabond, the despised and rejected—was her son's child, her grandson! The blood that flowed in his veins was hers—he was her very own, and she had driven him away to ruin, and, perhaps, to death!

It was an awful moment for her. Pride and composure were forgotten; she was very human and weak in her remorse and sorrow. With a cry of distress that brought Mrs. Ainsworth to the room, she threw herself back in her chair and burst into tears.

"What is it? Oh, what has happened?" cried Mrs. Ainsworth in terror; she had never seen the stately old lady weep, and the sight of her sorrow was extremely touching.

"Laura, oh, Laura, how can I ever forgive myself?" she exclaimed, when she saw bending over her the pale, pitying face of her daughter-in-law. "What can we do? How can we find him? That boy, that child that I have driven away, is Philip's son—my poor Philip's son."

"What? Who?" interrupted Mrs. Ainsworth, wildly. She thought the old lady had suddenly gone insane.

But Madam Ainsworth did not heed the interruption nor the question. "Oh, I am fearfully punished," she went on excitedly. "There are all the certificates—the letters. Look at them; read them. They tell everything; they are as clear as day. See what I have brought upon myself. I was proud, cold, wicked; I would not listen to the pleadings of my heart. I *felt* for that child. I had to struggle with myself not to love him. It was the old bitter prejudice, the hatred for what had caused the sorrow of my life. If he had come from any other place on earth I might have done him justice; but I said, like those of old, 'Can there anything good come out of Nazareth?' and I rejected him, although something told me that there was a tie between us. Oh, I felt it that day when I was cruel to him; when he pleaded so pitifully for his little pets. It was the very tone of voice, the very expression, of my Philip, when I used to reprove him for some childish fault. Poor little soul, I pitied him; but I almost broke his heart and my own with my stubborn pride."

"'WHAT IS IT? OH, WHAT HAS HAPPENED?' CRIED MRS. AINSWORTH."

While Madam Ainsworth was pouring out her bitter self-accusations, Mrs. Ainsworth was looking over the letters and papers with a puzzled, bewildered air. "Oh," she said at length, "it must be true; he must be Captain Ainsworth's child. Edward felt it when he first saw him. It was the resemblance to his brother that made him love the boy; he told me so then; and besides, he was so like *our boy*. I was always surprised that you could not see the resemblance." And Mrs. Ainsworth wiped away the tears that filled her eyes. "But what can we do? How can we find him?" And she looked helplessly at her mother-in-law, who was making a desperate effort to recover her composure.

"I must write to Edward at once; he must leave that business and come to us," replied Madam Ainsworth, decidedly. "What does it matter whether we lose or gain money while Philip's child is drifting about the world exposed to want and sin? Laura, while I am writing to Edward send for that detective. We must give him more money; we must make greater efforts; the child can and must be found. Until I see him again I can never know peace or happiness. My son will reproach me from his grave, and I shall reproach myself as long as I live. There is no time to be lost; we must begin this very moment."

And the ardor and energy with which Madam Ainsworth put her plans into execution furnished a striking contrast to her former coldness and indifference.

CHAPTER XXXI

THEY PRESS ON

THE two little pilgrims did not remain long in Washington. Lilybel's enormous appetite for sweets, and his fondness for sight-seeing, very soon depleted Philip's pocket-book, which could not be replenished by exhibiting the "children," as the little negro had proposed, for Philip was aware that the little cage of white mice would furnish a certain means of identifying them; so he kept them carefully covered, and seldom allowed them to be seen. And he decided in the future to avoid large cities,—they offered too many temptations to Lilybel,—and to confine himself to country roads and obscure villages.

So they set forth again, as bright and hopeful as at first, and drifted on, sometimes a wind of chance blowing them in the right direction, sometimes in the wrong. Still they progressed slowly but surely toward their destination. They were not so fortunate in getting "lifts" as Lilybel had predicted, but they had seldom suffered for food and shelter. Lilybel's tin bucket, which he clung to through all vicissitudes, had usually contained something eatable upon which they could fall back in an emergency. When some generous housewife would give them more than they could eat at one meal, the remainder went into the bucket to furnish subsistence on a long march from one point of supply to another.

As they went south the weather became milder, and they did not suffer much from cold. Very early in the march Lilybel and his shoes parted company, which was no hardship to the little darky, whose feet were as tough as leather and as hard as bone. But Philip, after being daintily shod for so long, when obliged to part with his foot-covering suffered terribly from blisters and wounds caused by constantly tramping over rough roads. At times, when he found it impossible to take another step, he would sit down disheartened and declare he could go no farther. Then Lilybel would encourage him by telling him that he "saw er smoke," or "heard er train"; therefore they must be near a house or a railroad where they could rest and procure assistance. Then Philip, very pale and with compressed lips, would struggle up and press on; and if he failed utterly, Lilybel would supplement the exhausted physical force by carrying his companion on his back, with a sturdy determination and strength wonderful in such a mite.

But Philip was very thin and light. In fact, he seemed to *wilt* away day by day until, as he sometimes said laughingly, there was nothing of him but clothes, and these too were beginning to wilt; a hole here, a rent there, a tatter left on a bush, a scrap jagged off by pushing through a hedge or climbing a rude fence, told him that soon his garments would be in the condition of Lilybel's.

If Madam Ainsworth could have caught a glimpse of Philip after six weeks of wandering, her opinion that he was a vagabond would have been fully confirmed by his appearance. But in spite of the hardships endured by the little pilgrims, Père Josef's "children" fared sumptuously every day. They had plenty to eat, they were warm, and well cared for, and, on the whole, preferred swinging along over the road, with occasional glimpses of sunlight and blue skies, to being shut up in a close, dim room, and they were as merry as ever; they played their little games, and performed their sprightly tricks readily and often, and often furnished their small share to the general fund by bringing in coppers and nickels, which Lilybel delighted to collect in his cap, after the manner of itinerant showmen; and the farther they went South the more frequent these exhibitions became, until they were rarely without small sums of money; but owing to Lilybel's fondness for luxuries and contempt for essentials, they never could get enough ahead to supply themselves with all necessities. However, they drifted on, laughing one day, and crying the next; overfed at one meal, and hungry for days together; one night cold, with only the skies for a covering, another housed under some hospitable roof.

When Philip asked for shelter and food he was seldom refused. The pretty, gentle little fellow, with his droll black companion, excited interest in every one; and when some, curious to know the why of this peculiar partnership, questioned Philip, he would smilingly reply, "Oh, he's my friend." And that was all the information he would give.

One night darkness overtook them among the mountains of Tennessee. It was in April, but it was keenly cold on the hills. The stars glittered brightly;

the air was full of frost; the dry branches and leaves crackled and rustled around them. They were on a mountain road climbing toilsomely up and up, and they did not know just where they were; but they were confident that if they kept to the highway it would lead to some place. At last they could go no farther, and they sat down in the dark quite exhausted. They were cold and hungry, and, unfortunately, Lilybel's bucket was empty.

After resting for a few moments, they drew some dead leaves and branches together under the shelter of a tree, and with the "children" between them, they lay down in their little nest quite contentedly. Scarcely had they composed themselves to sleep when they heard something among the bushes cautiously approaching them; a soft, regular tramp, a rustling of leaves, and then a certain slow measured breathing; some living thing was very near them.

Lilybel started up in terror, and his eyes gleamed white in the darkness. "A b'ar! It's a b'ar!" he cried, scrambling for his life up the tree. "Cum, quick!— cum!" he called back to Philip. "Cum quick, er he'll cotch yer an' eat yer."

"I can't; how can I climb a tree with the 'children'? And I won't leave them," replied Philip, resolutely.

"It's a b'ar fer shore; I done heard him growl," insisted Lilybel.

"Oh, nonsense!" said Philip, skeptically. "I've got a match, and I'm going to see just what it is."

At that moment a large dark form was visible amid the bushes, and a warm breath swept over the boy's cheek. He struck the match and waited for it to blaze; then he exclaimed joyfully, "It's a cow! It's only a cow."

"Is it er-chawin' gum?" asked Lilybel, cautiously, "'Ca'se if it's er-chawin' gum it's er tame cow, an' I ain't afeard."

"It's chewing something," said Philip. "Come down; it isn't going to hurt you."

"Not if it's er *tame* cow," replied Lilybel, coming down more slowly than he went up. "Let's make er fire so 's I can see, an' I'll milk her. I knows how ter milk er *tame* cow."

But Philip had no more matches, and they lay down again to wait for morning, with the gentle, motherly creature near them. It gave Philip a feeling of safety and comfort, and he would soon have been asleep had not Lilybel begun to whimper with the cold: "I 's mos' froze; I 's mos' dade."

"Here, take my coat," said Philip; "I'm not very cold."

"No, I won't, Mars' Philip; you 's sick, an' you 's col' too. I won't take yer coat."

Perhaps Lilybel was beginning to understand dimly something of the beauty of unselfishness; for he complained no more, but burrowed deeper into his nest of leaves, and was soon sleeping soundly. Then Philip softly removed his coat,—he had a jacket under it,—and laid it over the little negro, and tucked it around him gently; after which he nestled down with his arm around the little cage, and slept a restless, feverish sleep.

"PHILIP GRIEVED SORELY OVER THE TINY DEAD THING."

When he awoke it was dawn, and he was benumbed with cold; his feet and hands ached pitifully, his head throbbed and whirled, and for a moment he felt that he could not stand up; but at last, with a great effort, he got upon his feet, and shook off the weakness which was daily gaining on him.

The gentle cow was still near them, and Lilybel was soon drawing into his tin bucket a generous stream of warm milk, of which they drank freely. When they had taken all they wished, the practical little negro filled the bucket for future use.

This grateful beverage refreshed and cheered Philip, and he was about to start forth more hopefully; but, to his surprise and distress, when he uncovered the cage of the "children" he found poor little Boule-de-Neige lying stark and dead. She was always more delicate than the others, and in spite of her name, the tender little sprite had succumbed to the cold. It was the first accident to the "children," and Philip grieved sorely over the tiny dead thing. He could not bear to leave it behind, so he put it within his jacket, hoping the warmth might revive it; and after protecting the others as well as he could, the little pilgrims set forth on their wearisome journey with heavy, sorrowful hearts.

CHAPTER XXXII

THE SWEET-OLIVE IS IN BLOOM

IT was the time of the sweet-olive and jasmine when the little pilgrims neared their journey's end. For fully two months they had been on their wearisome way, and every day their difficulties and sufferings had increased because of Philip's failing strength.

Exposure, hunger, and cold had done their work on the delicate frame of the boy, until he grew so thin and wan that one looking at him would have said that his days were numbered. Toward the last it was almost impossible for him to walk any distance without resting; he complained of feeling tired and sleepy, but never hungry, and had it not been for the kind country people who gave them a "lift" now and then on their carts, and the good-natured conductors on the different freight-trains, who helped them along from one place to another, Philip would have fallen by the way, and his weary little body would have been left behind asleep in some obscure grave. In spite of the boy's physical weakness his moral courage never failed; he was as hopeful, as confident, as cheerful as when they first set forth. Sometimes he would start out with feverish energy. "I'm not sick," he would say resolutely; "I'm only tired, and we *must* go on." For a little distance, while the excitement lasted, he would press forward eagerly, but suddenly his strength would fail and he would sit down by the wayside exhausted and faint.

Then Lilybel would use every argument to encourage him to make another effort. Sometimes it would be a smoke, or the distant sound of a cow-bell, or the rumbling of wheels, and when these signs failed and Philip did not respond to Lilybel's allurements, the sturdy little negro, whose greatest virtue was his fidelity, would take up his frail burden and trudge on until he reached the assistance that he had predicted.

In this way they progressed, slowly and wearily, until at last one night found them near the shore of the lovely lake which stretched, an impassable barrier, between them and their promised land. It was May; a great round moon as bright as a silver shield shone above them. They were in a forest of pines; the wind soughed and murmured among the boughs; the air was sweet with the resinous odor of the sap that flowed from the wounded trees; the earth was strewn with the fragrant needles of the pine until it was as soft and soothing as the most luxurious bed.

When Philip, exhausted from his day's struggle, stretched his suffering little body on the friendly earth, it was with a feeling of thankfulness that he had made his last march, that the journey was over; for he thought the soughing of the wind among the trees was the murmuring of the lake, that they were on its very shores, and had but to cross its sparkling waters, when in truth it lay flashing in the moonbeams miles and miles away. He was very ill that night; his face was flushed and hot with fever, and his eyes were large and bright when he raised them to Lilybel, who sat beside him crying in his low, whimpering way.

"What are you crying for, Lilybel?" asked Philip, dreamily. He seemed to be floating up and up among the trees toward the silver shield of the moon.

"I's er-cryin' 'ca'se yer sick, Mars' Philip, an' wes can't git ercross der lake. Now wes yere we can't git ercross. Wes can't *walk* ercross dat water, and New 'leens is jes' on de oder side, an' wes can't git ercross 'ca'se wes can't walk," repeated Lilybel, dolefully.

"No," said Philip, "we can't walk any more, but we can stay here and rest. We can stay here always."

"No, we can't stay here, Mars' Philip; wes got ter git ercross," returned Lilybel, decidedly.

"It's like Mammy's garden," murmured Philip. His mind wandered, as he drifted off into a feverish sleep.

"But hit 's a mighty long way from dar, an' wes got ter git ercross," still insisted Lilybel.

"The sweet-olive 's in bloom; I smell it, and the jasmine, too."

"No, Mars' Philip, it ain't no sweet-olive; dar ain't none yere. It's jes dem piney-trees what yer smells."

"Dea, let's go to Rue Royale before the sweet-olive withers."

"What yer talkin' erbout, Mars' Philip? Yer can't go ter Rue Royale till yer cross der lake," and Lilybel bent over the sick boy and looked into his face with eyes full of alarm. "He's ersleep, an' he's dreamin' out loud. My, my! he's awful sick; he's got der fever. An' how's I er-gwine ter git him ercross der lake?"

Suddenly Lilybel ducked his head and listened. Then he lay down flat and put his ear to the earth. "Dat's er train, shore, and it's over dar. It ain't fur, an' it's er train what's gwine ter cross der lake. My, my! if wes war on dat track wes 'd git took over, shore. Dey'd take on a boy what's sick an' mos' dade. He's got der fever an' he's er-dreamin' out loud. Dey'd take him on, an' I 's got ter git him dar. I 's got ter wake him. Cum, Mars' Philip, yer's got ter git on my back; I 's got ter tote yer."

But Lilybel spoke to deaf ears. Philip was in a deep stupor, unconscious of pain or weariness, and when the little negro lifted the heavy head it fell back inertly on its pillow of pine-needles.

"It ain't no use—he won't wake; I 's got ter tote him like er baby, an' dem little mices, too. I 's got ter tote dem on my back, an' Mars' Philip in my arms."

"TAKING PHILIP IN HIS ARMS, HE TRUDGED OFF
TOWARD A LARGE TREE."

There is no undergrowth in these pine-forests; one can see long distances through the vista of trees, and Lilybel, later on, caught the faint flash of a light and heard again the rumble of a train. This decided him in what direction to go; so he arranged his burdens as he best could, and, taking Philip in his arms as tenderly as he would a sleeping infant, he trudged off toward a large tree which stood, stripped of bark, bare and white in the moonlight.

The little negro, burdened as he was, could not walk far without stopping to recover his breath; therefore, when he came to a favorable spot, he would put Philip gently down and sit beside him until he was sufficiently rested to be able to lift him up and push on a little farther, with careful steps and eyes fixed on his landmark, shining whiter and more distinct the nearer he approached it.

This difficult and tedious performance occupied a greater part of the night, and, much to Lilybel's joy, when the morning dawned he found himself in a clearing, and only a few paces from a railroad. When it was light enough for him to see a little distance ahead, he also discovered that he was near a water-station.

"Now wes safe," he said, exultingly. "Dey's got ter stop yere to water der ingine, an' I's only got ter git Mars' Philip up by dat tank an' wait till der train cums erlong."

This feat, which was nothing compared to what he had accomplished through the night, was easily performed, and when Philip awoke at last from his long, heavy sleep, he found himself lying on the grass in the shadow of the water-tank, and Lilybel sitting beside him, bathing his face and hands with cool, sweet water.

"I done tole yer wes near der railroad," said the little negro, delightedly, when Philip sat up and looked around him with surprise.

"Where are we? Have we crossed the lake?" asked Philip, still confused and a little dizzy.

"No, wes ain't crossed yit, but wes gwine ter on der fust train what cums erlong."

"How did I get here, Lilybel?" questioned Philip. "I went to sleep under a pine-tree, and I don't remember waking."

"No, yer didn't wake; I done toted yer while yer wuz asleep," replied Lilybel, proudly.

"And the 'children,' too?"

"Yes, der mices, too," returned Lilybel, with satisfaction.

Philip smiled and laid down contentedly. In a few moments he was asleep again, while Lilybel sat beside him, patiently watching him. At last he awoke, greatly refreshed. The fever was gone and his head was clear, but he was very weak.

It was getting on toward noon, and Lilybel looked and listened for the train which he was sure would come.

"I hears it now, Mars' Philip," or "I sees er smoke," was the constant encouraging remark to which Philip listened, a gentle smile on his lips and his eyes full of expectation.

But at last, at last, they heard a distant rumble, then a rushing and a snorting, and a heavy freight-train hove in sight. It was a moment of intense anxiety for the little pilgrims. Would it slow up at the water-tank, or would it not? Philip forgot his weakness, and tottered to his feet. Lilybel stood perilously near the track, and waved his tattered cap. The great thirsty monster came swiftly on, glaring at them with its bright eye, snorting and puffing, slower and slower. "Yas, yas, it's er-gwine ter stop!" shouted Lilybel. "Yas, it's *done* stopped." And, sure enough, with many a jolt and shiver, the long train drew up before the water-tank, and the men jumped out and proceeded to quench the thirst of the fiery dragon.

When the conductor saw the little tattered figure of Lilybel standing near the tank, he laughed and said: "Hello, scarecrow! where did you come from? What you doin' here?" Then noticing Philip, who was leaning feebly against the side of the tank, he said, not unkindly: "Here's another, a white one, an' sick, too, I guess."

Philip lifted his eyes and smiled; the gentle, friendly smile went straight to the man's heart. "Waiting for the train, eh? Want to board it to cross the lake?"

"If you please, sir?" replied Philip, eagerly. "I'm sick; I can't walk any more."

"I guess you can't," returned the conductor, lifting the boy gently; "yer about used up. How far have ye footed it?"

"From Chattanooga," said Philip, evasively.

"Ye have, have ye? Well, no wonder yer nothin' but skin and bones. Yes, get in; I'll cross yer."

"And him, too?" indicating Lilybel.

"The little scarecrow? Oh, he can get in; the two of you won't weigh more 'n a cat. Here, Bill," he called to the brakeman, "can't yer fix up something for this young one? He looks as if he'd faint away. Don't b'lieve he's had anything to eat for a week. Frogged it from Chattanooga. Just think of that!"

"Plenty o' pluck fer such a bundle o' bones. Yes, I'll git him something," replied the brakeman, looking kindly at the boy. "Most starved, ain't ye?"

"No, I'm not hungry, thank you," returned Philip, still smiling; "I'm only thirsty."

"Thirsty! Well, I'll make ye a drink in two winks," and turning to a shelf, he drained some black coffee from a can into a mug, and then taking a small flask from his pocket, he poured something from it into the coffee, and putting in some sugar, he stirred it well.

"Here, my little man, drink this, an' it'll set you up," he said cheerily, giving the mug to Philip. "It's greased lightnin'. It'll cure you right off. You'll be well afore ye git across."

Philip drank the black draught greedily, and lay down contentedly on the hard seat of the caboose, while Lilybel sat beside him and munched some corn bread and bacon supplied by the generous brakeman.

While the train rolled on toward the lake, Philip lay looking through the open door of the caboose. Suddenly he cried, "Oh, there's latania and cypress! I see the moss waving in the wind. We're in Louisiana, aren't we?"

"Yes, we crossed the line away back; we're near the lake, and we'll be in New Orleans in an hour or so."

At the sound of the magic words, Philip brightened instantly. He was well and strong now; he sat up and looked eagerly to catch the first glimpse of the lake; he was all excitement, all energy. "So near, so near," he whispered to Lilybel. "Oh, there's the lake; how wide, how blue, how beautiful! It is like sailing on the sea." And while he chattered and laughed, the train rolled over the long bridge across the shining, placid water of the beautiful lake.

CHAPTER XXXIII

AFTER MANY DAYS

WHEN the train pulled into the station, Philip could hardly wait for it to stop, so eager was he to get off. "We will go to Rue Royale and find Seline first," he said joyously to Lilybel, who suddenly seemed much subdued, and not so elated as one should be over the termination of so many difficulties and untoward adventures.

"I spects my ma 's gwine ter beat me fur runnin' erway. I 's mos' feared to go dar; I guess I'll go on der levee fust, an' wait ter see ef she's er-gwine ter beat me."

"Seline won't do anything of the kind," returned Philip, confidently. "She'll be too glad to see you. Come on, and I'll see that she doesn't scold you."

"My ma she t'inks I 's dade," said Lilybel, still doubtful of his welcome; "an' I s'pects she'll be mad if I cums ter life."

Philip laughed his old merry laugh. "Oh, come on, and don't be afraid. Seline's so good she won't hurt you." With hasty thanks to the kind trainmen, he almost flew out of the station, into Elysian Fields, and up Rue Royale, scarcely stopping to take breath as he hurried along. He was no longer a little soiled, dejected pilgrim; he did not think of his weakness, his ragged, dusty garments, his tangled hair and grimy skin. After many days of hope deferred, of pain, weariness, and anxiety, he was once more Toinette's Philip, running up Rue Royale to find Seline.

At the cathedral close he stopped a moment to look into the garden. How lovely it was! Yes, there was the sweet-olive in bloom, the jasmine dotted with white stars, the borders purple with violets. Pressing his thin face against the iron railings, he breathed in the familiar perfume greedily. "Oh, it's lovely to be home," he said, beaming with smiles; "and what will Seline say? Won't she be surprised to see us!"

So confident was Philip of finding Seline in her old place, that the possibility of her not being there had never occurred to him, and even when he reached the very portico of the old bank and saw no trace of her, or of her stand, he could not believe his eyes, but stood staring in blank amazement at the vacant spot, the place where she always sat smiling a welcome the moment he came within her line of vision. But now there was nothing there, absolutely nothing, that belonged to her. The stately columns, the fine portico, were dwarfed and mean without Seline. The place seemed wretchedly dreary and empty, and the cold gray stone struck a chill to his heart.

"Where's my ma?" gasped Lilybel, his eyes starting out with surprise. "She's done gone; she ain't yere," and he gave a sigh, half of relief—the chance of punishment was again deferred.

Philip said nothing; he could find no words to express his disappointment. Brushing away the hot tears, he entered a shop near the bank and made inquiries for Seline. In the old days every one in the neighborhood knew Seline; but this was a new tenant; he had been there only a year, and he had never seen a stand under the portico of the old building in all that time. Philip went out discouraged and asked the same anxious questions at several other places. Oh, yes, the old colored woman; she hadn't been there for a year or more; they couldn't say where she had gone. That was all the information he could get.

"I s'pects my ma's dade," whimpered Lilybel. He could see no other possible reason for her abandoning her old stand.

"Oh, don't say that," cried Philip, sharply. "She isn't dead; she's only gone away, and we must find her." Then pulling himself together, he tried to meet this unexpected emergency with courage.

After a moment's silence, he said, quite cheerfully, to Lilybel: "You go to Seline's house and see if she's there, and if she isn't there, try to find out where she is, and I'll go to St. Mary's and ask if Père Josef has got back. I'll wait there for you on the steps. Hurry as fast as you can, and bring Seline with you."

Lilybel did not stand upon the order of his going, but scuttled off as fast as he could to do Philip's bidding; besides, he too was somewhat anxious to know what had become of his ma.

After he had gone, Philip retraced his steps, a forlorn little figure in the bright spring sunshine. When he passed the cathedral on his way to St. Mary's, he did not notice the flowers nor the fragrance of the garden; his head was bent dejectedly and his step was slow and feeble.

At the entrance of the church, he waited for a priest who was coming out,—a gentle-looking old man. Philip stopped him, and, with a quaver in his voice, asked if Père Josef had returned.

"Père Josef! Oh, no; he isn't back, but he's expected—he's expected any day," and with a glance of mild curiosity at the tattered boy the priest passed out.

Philip's face was radiant in a moment. "Any day, any day," he repeated. "Well, perhaps he'll come to-day. I'll sit on the steps and wait for Lilybel, and it may be that he'll come while I'm waiting."

Père Josef did not come, but after a while Lilybel hove in sight, breathless and excited. "Her ain't dade," he cried, as soon as he was within hearing distance; "but her ain't dar nudder. A colored lady tole me her 's done move erway more 'n a year, an' she don't know whar her's gone; she s'pects her 's gone ter der country. I's bin on der levee, an' one of dem luggers is er-gwine up der ruver ter-night, an' I's er-gwine ter go on her ter find my ma fer yer, Mars' Philip, an' I's gwine ter bring her back. Dat lady she guv me some biscuit and fried chicken, an' I 's brought it to you, 'ca'se I'll git plenty ter eat on dat lugger. An' Mars' Philip, yer jes' wait yere till I come back with my ma."

That night, when the old sacristan of the Archbishop's palace was closing the gates of the garden, he found a forlorn little figure curled up on the grass in a corner, sound asleep, with one arm clasped tightly around a small bundle.

"Some poor little wanderer," thought the old man. "I won't disturb him; he can't do any harm here. I'll let him sleep." And so Philip was left to dream away the night in the Archbishop's garden, under the shadow of St. Mary's Church.

As soon as it was light, he was awake; and, without waiting to say *bon jour* to the old sacristan, he sallied forth, weak in body, but strong in heart. With the morning had come the determination to find Dea. He knew she lived on Villeré street, but he had never been there, and was not certain of the exact locality. Still, he thought he could find her by inquiring from door to door.

On his way to Villeré street he stopped to look in his Mammy's old garden. It was very early, and there was no one near to witness his surprise when he saw how the place was changed. The stucco of the wall was repaired and freshly colored, the iron scrollwork of the gate was as bright and fresh as new paint could make it. The vagrant vines no longer trailed over the walls, the

Pittosporum trees were carefully trimmed, and the walks and borders newly cleaned. And there, in front of Toinette's little cottage, was a pretty, graceful house, new and white, with slender columns, deep galleries, and cool, shady awnings. Was it possible that this was the old neglected garden? It is true there were the broken white pillars with their masses of verdure, the oaks and magnolias, and the rose-garden fresh and blooming. But where was his Mammy? Where were the Major and the Singer? They were gone, and strangers were there. It was no longer his home. With a heart-breaking sob he turned away, and hastened down Ursulines street toward Villeré.

For some time he wandered up and down, meeting with no success. He could not find any one who had ever heard of the artist in wax; but at last, when he was almost discouraged, he stopped at a cottage and obtained some information. "Yes, it was in the very next house that they lived,—an artist and his little daughter; but they were gone. A strange monsieur came and took them away a long time ago. And it was said that they had gone to France."

"HE LEANED AGAINST THE FENCE OF THE DESERTED COTTAGE, AND CRIED BITTERLY."

This was the most unexpected and the most crushing blow of all. He had never thought of it; but what was more likely than that Dea's rich uncle had taken them away with him? For some time he leaned against the fence of the deserted cottage, and cried bitterly. He was getting very weak and hopeless now. Then he took up his little bundles and went away, slowly and dejectedly, back to St. Mary's Church, his last and only asylum.

And while Philip sat waiting on the steps of the church, tired and ill and seemingly deserted by all, in New York his nearest of kin, almost as discouraged and hopeless as he, were using every means that wealth and influence could command, and that repentant, anxious hearts could dictate, to discover the homeless, suffering boy.

CHAPTER XXXIV

AT THE GATE

SEVERAL days had passed since his arrival, and Philip still lingered around St. Mary's, waiting for Père Josef and Lilybel. He had seen Père Martin pass in and out several times, but he had not made himself known, because he remembered that Mr. Ainsworth was in correspondence with the priest of St. Mary's, and that through him they might learn of his return to New Orleans; and Père Josef's friend did not recognize Toinette's Philip in the sickly, tattered boy who lingered so persistently around the steps of the church.

After a day or two the old sacristan became interested in the child, and offered him food, and even a pallet to sleep on in one corner of his little room in the lodge at the gate of the Archbishop's palace. He saw that the boy was ill, and that he had not always been the neglected little vagrant that he appeared to be; and his anxious, pathetic inquiries for Père Josef, who was one of the sacristan's favorites, added to the pity he felt for the boy.

Every night as Philip entered the lodge he would ask the same question in such a sad and patient voice that the old man almost wept.

"Do you think Père Josef will come to-morrow, Mr. Sacristan?"

And the sacristan would answer, as cheerfully as he could, *"Oui, mon enfant,* I think he will come to-morrow."

With a great deal of mystery, and many hints as to the necessity of secrecy, being so near his reverence the Archbishop, Philip had uncovered the little cage and showed Père Josef's "children" to the sacristan, and he had almost forgotten his troubles and disappointments to laugh with the old man over their droll tricks.

One night he was very ill again: he had fever, and dreamed out loud, as Lilybel said. All night he talked and talked, sitting up on his pallet with wide, bright eyes and smiling lips. His delirium did not take the form of stupor, as it had that memorable night in the pine-forest. He was happy, even merry: he laughed over his little tricks with the poor "doll"; he called the sacristan Mr. Butler, and chatted with him as he had with Bassett in the time of their pleasant companionship; he lived over the brightest days of his life,—the later and darker period, his dreary pilgrimage, and even his recent disappointment seemed all forgotten.

The old sacristan, alarmed at his high fever, his restlessness and delirium, sat by his little pallet all night, gave him copious draughts of fresh water, and tenderly bathed his burning hands and face. Toward morning the fever left him, and he sank into a deep, refreshing sleep. When he awoke, the sacristan and the priest to whom he had spoken on the day of his arrival were bending over him. They were talking in a low voice, and he heard them repeat the word "hospital" several times. They were going to send him to the hospital; he was very ill; he must go where he could have proper care.

The hospital!—to Philip that meant only one thing: it was a place where people were sent to die; when once they entered there they never came out—except to be carried to their last resting-place. He was very ill, but he could not die before Père Josef and Lilybel came back,—no; he could not go to the hospital. He said nothing, but lay very quiet until the priest and the sacristan went out. As soon as they disappeared within the church, he got up, and, taking his little bundle, tottered feebly into the street.

The glare of the sun hurt his head; he felt faint and weak, but he hastened on down Ursulines street out of sight of the palace and St. Mary's Church. He could stay there no longer; that last asylum was closed to him. If he went back, he would be sent to the hospital, and he would never see Père Josef and Lilybel. Lilybel would be sure to come with Seline; they would look for him on the steps of St. Mary's, and he would not be there, and they would never know where to find him.

This last calamity was almost overwhelming; but he must not give up, he must keep on his feet, because if he fell in the street, he would be picked up and sent to the hospital, and then what would become of the "children"? Some one might steal them, or they might get lost, if he were taken away from them. Then he thought of St. Roch's. If it were not so far! If he could only get there—there on his Mammy's grave, surely no one would disturb him! But the hospital!—the hospital!—kept ringing in his ears. He could not, he must not, go there.

When he was far enough from St. Mary's to feel somewhat safe, he found a shady doorway, and sat down to rest and consider what he should do; but he could not think, his head whirled strangely, everything seemed moving, even the street and the houses; then he felt sleepy, and was about to close his eyes when a rough voice smote his ear:

"Git out er dat, you young one; I 's er-gwine ter clean dese steps an' dis yere banquette." And, looking up, Philip saw a stout negress, with a pail of water and a broom, waiting to begin her work.

Philip staggered to his feet and went on down Ursulines street blindly and dizzily, like one in a dream. It seemed to him that he had walked miles when, without knowing how he had come there, he suddenly became aware that he was again before the Detrava place.

The great oaks on each side of the entrance made a dense shade. It had rained during the night, and a sweet, moist odor filled the air. Again Philip lingered and looked in through the iron scrollwork. He was so weak and tired that he could not stand, so he sat down before the gate, and, resting against the stone post, looked up into the great waving branches above him. There were birds hopping about among the leaves; yes, there were a mocking-bird and a cardinal, and innumerable little brown birds. Suddenly the mocking-bird broke into a clear liquid strain, and, spreading its wings, soared away into the distant sky. Philip watched it dreamily. Was it the Singer? He was not sure, but oh, how he wished he could follow its flight into that infinite, restful blue!

How fresh and dewy the garden looked! What enchanting fragrance,— what soft shadows among the waving vines! It was like looking into Paradise. If they would only open the gate and allow him to enter and lie down in the shade under his favorite tree! It was there still; he could see it, and he could see people moving on the shady galleries; and in the rose-garden a tall, dark man was walking back and forth. In his hand he held a book, but oftener he looked up at the sky, as if his treasures were there.

While Philip strained his eyes to watch the man, he suddenly saw appear on the gallery a radiant white figure. It was a young girl or an angel, he could not tell which; then a stout colored woman came in sight and handed the radiant creature a nosegay of white flowers tied with trailing white ribbons, and a small white book, which the young girl took in a grave, gentle way; then, with graceful, sedate steps, she slowly descended to the garden, followed by the woman and a large, serious-looking old dog.

At the entrance of the rose-garden the man met the gracious young creature, and, lifting the cloud of net from over her face, he stooped and kissed her gravely and tenderly. Then the little procession came on down the walk, the girl stepping daintily in her white shoes, while she held her cloud of lace away from the intruding roses that would fain caress her. She was surely no mortal. To Philip, in his bewildered condition, she seemed a spirit, a radiant creature from another world.

The slender white-robed figure, with its misty veil and crown of white flowers, seemed to float and float toward him.

Was he dreaming? or was he already dead, and was it a sweet vision of eternity? It was surely Dea's face under the veil; it was surely Dea's soft grave smile that he saw, her low gentle voice that he heard. And the woman behind her was Seline—yes, Seline. And the dog? Why, the dog was Homo! And they were at the gate—at the very gate; if he could stretch out his hand he could touch them! He heard the key rattle in the lock, the old gate creak and slowly open, and in a voice that seemed to reach to heaven he cried, "Dea! Seline!" and fell feebly forward into a pair of strong arms stretched out to receive him. From a long murmuring distance he heard a soft voice say, "It is Philip; yes, it is Philip." And he felt himself clasped and carried away—away, he knew not whither, for he drifted into blissful rest, while faintly and dimly he heard the rustling of leaves, and the far-off singing of birds.

CHAPTER XXXV

A BED OF ROSES

WHEN Dea, white-robed and fair as an angel, stepping daintily forth to her first communion, saw the little emaciated and tattered figure at the gate, she did not recognize in it her former merry little friend. But the cry, "Dea! Seline!" was enough. In an instant she was beside him, and while Seline received the fainting boy in her strong arms, it was Dea who took his dusty, tangled head to her heart, in spite of her cloud of lace and dainty white frock, and it was Dea's tears and kisses he felt on his forehead as he drifted away into blissful unconsciousness.

This meeting was not the meeting that Dea had looked forward to. For months and months she had been expecting Philip, and she always thought of him as she had last seen him—happy, healthy, and full of the excitement of his expected journey. But he was none the less welcome; the fact that he was ill and suffering, and needed her, made him still dearer.

When her uncle, after vainly trying to induce his brother to return with him to France, took possession of the Detrava place and built the pretty house they now occupied, Dea asked that the cottage and Philip's room might remain just as they were, so that when he returned he would find everything as he had left it; and when Seline, after her bereavement,—for she believed that Lilybel, contrary to her prediction, had been "drownded in der ruver,"— decided to give up her stand and retire to private life as Dea's housekeeper, she and her adored little ma'mselle took pleasure in beautifying the room and keeping it fresh and sweet for the boy they both loved so dearly. Therefore, when Philip recovered from his swoon and opened his eyes, he found himself lying on his own little white bed, which seemed to him a bed of roses, so soft and sweet was it; and Seline, her dusky face wet with tears, was bending over him tenderly, while Dea, still in her white frock, rubbed and stroked his thin brown hands.

For some moments Philip said nothing, but lay contentedly smiling up in their faces. Then he asked if Lilybel had come.

At the mention of that name, Seline, with a sob, turned her head away; she felt all a mother's sorrow at the loss of her troublesome black lamb. "Oh, Mars' Philip, yer don't know, does yer, dat my poor Lilybel's 'ceased more 'n a year ago?—dat he was done drownded in der ruver?"

"No, he wasn't, Seline," cried Philip, struggling to sit up and shake off his weakness: he had so much to tell, so much to hear, that he could not lie there dull and silent. Then he told Seline, briefly, and in a weak but happy voice, of the prodigal's return, not from a watery grave, but from New York, to which Dea and the old woman listened with many exclamations of surprise and joy.

"An' jes' ter t'ink," said Seline, laughing and crying together, "I's be'n in deep mournin' fer dat boy fer more 'n a year, an' now I's got ter take it off— an' my bes' dress ain't near wore out!"

While Philip was feebly recounting some of their adventures, there was a rustling and rattling at the door, and Lilybel himself entered, escorted by Homo, who had recognized his old companion, and had received him with the dignity becoming a dog whose condition had greatly improved.

There was a very affecting meeting between Lilybel and his mother, at which Dea and Philip smiled through their tears.

"An' how did yer fine out whar I war?" asked Seline, when she had recovered herself a little.

"Dat cousin in der country done tole me; an' when I couldn't fine Mars' Philip on dem church steps dis mawnin', I jes' come erlong down yere. An' Ma, now I ain't dade, I 's gwine ter be a good boy an' wuk right smart. I 's gwine ter help yer nuss Mars' Philip an' git him well, 'c'ase he's mighty sick; an'—an' I ain't nuver gwine ter run erway no more, 'c'ase I don't like dem steamboats, an' I don't like ter *walk* nudder."

On the strength of Lilybel's good resolutions, he was established in the Detrava household, where in time he became a useful and accomplished servant; and to Dea he was even something of a hero when she learned of his fidelity to Philip through that long and weary pilgrimage.

After Philip was bathed and clothed in clean white garments,— some of the very garments that he had given to Lilybel in the days of his prosperity, and which Seline had cherished as something precious,—he was laid back in his bed, and Mr. Detrava brought a doctor—the very doctor who had told Philip that Toinette would never awake.

"He is very ill—very weak, but if we can break the fever, with good nursing and proper nourishment we may bring him around," said the doctor as he went away with Mr. Detrava, talking in a low, grave voice, while Philip lay smiling contentedly. He had reached his journey's end, he had found Dea and Seline, and it was so sweet to rest on his bed of roses in security and peace. After a while he fell asleep, and when he awoke he still smiled to see Dea and Seline sitting beside him, and the "children," on a little table near the window, scampering and playing merrily.

How quiet and pretty his old room was! how soft and soothing the sounds that came in through his open window: the singing of birds, the rustling of leaves! Never had a little pilgrim found such a flower-strewn path at his journey's end. Seline tended him as if he were an ailing infant, and Dea tempted his failing appetite with fresh fruits and delicious cooling drinks, and even the artist left the seclusion of his room to visit the sick boy.

Dea's father was no more companionable, none the less a dreamer than formerly; but he remembered Philip's kindness to his child in those old days of sorrow and poverty, and now he wished to show his gratitude in every possible way: he brought his lovely little figures to show the boy, for he still modeled industriously, although now he never sold his work, and his beautiful room was full of his exquisite productions. And Philip was interested and pleased with everything in a languid, mild way; he rarely showed any enthusiasm, any of his old fervor and excitement, over the things he liked. He slept a great deal, and complained only of being tired; sometimes he laughed softly, but the old merry ring had gone out of it. At times he spoke of the future, when he should be well, what he should do, and where he should go, but with little real interest. Often he had fever and talked incessantly of his wanderings and troubles, while Dea and Seline would listen with wet eyes and aching hearts. Had he not gone with those rich people to the cold North, he would have been well and happy—Toinette's merry Philip, instead of the feeble, wasted shadow before them.

One day, while he was sleeping lightly, he was awakened by a hot tear falling on his face, and, looking up, he saw Père Josef leaning over him. In a moment Philip's weak arms were around the priest's neck, and he was sobbing on his breast.

"LOOKING UP, HE SAW PÈRE JOSEF LEANING OVER HIM."

"*Mon enfant! mon enfant!*" was all Père Josef could say, as he stroked the wan cheek and soft hair.

As soon as Philip recovered his composure, he said regretfully, "I'm so sorry, Père Josef, but I couldn't help it—poor little Boule-de-Neige died of cold on the mountains. I carried her all day inside my jacket, but she never came to life, and I buried her under a tree, and put a little stone over her grave."

Père Josef smiled and brushed away a tear. "I never thought my 'children' would travel so far."

"But I brought the others back safely. I said I would take care of them, and I did as well as I could. I brought them back to you; there they are near the window."

"Yes, *mon enfant*, I have seen them. They are as gay and as charming as ever. You took very good care of them," returned Père Josef, stroking the little hot hand tenderly. "But we won't talk about the 'children' now; you are too ill, and there are many other things I must say to you—"

"I wanted to ask you a question before you went away," interrupted Philip, feebly; "but now it does not matter to know. I'm just Toinette's Philip, and it doesn't matter to know."

"But, my dear child, you *must* know; it is my duty to tell you. Will you lie there quietly and listen calmly while I tell you about your parents?"

"Yes, Père Josef, I will lie still and listen; but I'm Toinette's Philip all the same, and I always shall be."

Then Père Josef told him, as simply and briefly as he could, who his father and mother were, and of his future inheritance and expectations, to which Philip listened with languid indifference until the priest mentioned the name of Ainsworth; then he started up, flushed and excited. "No, no!" he cried; "I'm not Philip Ainsworth. I don't want the name; I don't want the money. Let Lucille and the baby have the money. I tried to be Philip Ainsworth; I tried to love them, and tried to make them love me, but they wouldn't. I heard Madam Ainsworth say that they didn't love me, and that they were tired of me; and that's why I ran away. I'm glad my real mama was a Detrava, and that Dea is some relation to me. I love Dea and Mr. Detrava, but I don't—I can't—love Madam Ainsworth after what she said."

"*Mon enfant*, she did not know that you were her grandson."

"But she might have loved me all the same. Mr. Butler Bassett loved me, and he said I wasn't a bad boy; but they didn't, and they never will. I've come back to be Toinette's Philip—just Toinette's Philip," he reiterated passionately.

Père Josef saw that in the boy's present condition it was useless to attempt to reason with him, so he only said soothingly, "You shall, you shall, *mon enfant;* calm yourself, and you shall be whatever you wish. It was my duty to tell you. Now it is over, and we won't talk of it any more."

"No, we won't talk of it or think of it," returned Philip, decidedly. "I am so happy, so contented, now, that the thought of going away where no one loves me gives me a pain here." And he laid his thin hand on his fluttering heart, and raised his eyes with such a pathetically appealing look in them that Père Josef almost regretted having performed his duty.

CHAPTER XXXVI

A Reconciliation

MR. AINSWORTH returned from the West as soon as possible after receiving his mother's urgent letter, and instituted without delay a systematic and thorough search for the missing boy. But their united and persistent efforts were as useless as the first attempt had been. Week after week passed in following up some clue which proved to be false, or waiting in anxious expectation for news from the different detectives they had employed throughout the country.

During those wearisome days of suspense, Madam Ainsworth aged visibly. She was less haughty and less severe, and she did not hesitate to confess to her friend that she could not sleep at night for thinking that the child might be wandering somewhere, tired and ill, and exposed to cold and hunger. At times she avoided the drawing-room, where Captain Ainsworth's portrait seemed to look at her reproachfully, his sad, persistent gaze following her everywhere. Then she would go into the boy's deserted room,—the room she had given him so grudgingly,—and opening his wardrobe she would look at its contents with an aching heart. The empty little garments had a pathos of their own. The warm fur coat that the boy had been so proud of, and liked so much to wear, was a keen rebuke to her when she thought that perhaps he was suffering with cold; and the pride which had prevented his taking their gifts told her too plainly that he had understood and resented their unkindness. Had she known that he was Philip's son, she would have made an idol of him: she would have been so proud of his beauty, of his fine manly bearing, of his frank, truthful nature, which she had discovered only when it was too late to show her appreciation of them.

It was a dreary time for her; even her new grandson failed to interest her, and the brilliant and mature expressions in Lucille's Paris letters were honored with only one hasty reading.

Mr. and Mrs. Ainsworth suffered too, but not so deeply as the old lady, because they were less guilty. In spite of their thoughtless neglect of Philip after the birth of their boy, they still loved their adopted son, and felt a real interest in him; and now that he was gone they missed him greatly, and were sadly anxious concerning him.

It had become a habit of the whole family, Bassett included, to expect with every sound of the door-bell, and every messenger, some news of the lost boy; and one day it came in a brief telegram, dated at New Orleans, and signed by Père Josef:

Philip is with his relatives, the Detravas, on Ursulines street. He is very ill.

Madam Ainsworth handed it to her son, her face pallid and sunken. "My punishment has just begun," she said brokenly, as she left the room. That night she and her son were on their way to New Orleans.

For several days after his conversation with Père Josef, Philip appeared to be better and brighter, and each day Seline lifted him from his bed and laid him in a large easy-chair near the window. From this comfortable position he could look into the garden and watch the gardener at work among the flowers.

He knew every tree and shrub, and the riotous vines running everywhere were a wonder to him. "Mammy planted that," he would say. "When I went away it wasn't up to my knee; now it's nearly as high as the house. It seems to be running up to the sky. I think it loves the stars and is trying to reach them. And there's the very magnolia-fuscata we set out one day—the day Père Josef went away. It was a little thing then; now it's nearly a tree. And that's the bed of lilies we planted the day Dea sold Quasimodo. And those violets in that border are the last dear Mammy put out; I helped her, and the Major and the Singer were around me all the time; and how the Singer trilled that day! I never heard him trill so before; perhaps he knew it was the last time Mammy would hear him. I wish the Singer would come back, but I think he and the Major are gone. They missed me, and they went away; perhaps they have gone to search for me, and when they can't find me they will come back."

Dea watched him constantly, with wistful, anxious eyes, hope and fear alternating. "He's better to-day," she would say confidently to Seline; but the old woman would only shake her head sorrowfully, and go away to wipe her eyes secretly.

One morning he was especially bright—almost merry; he played with the "children," caressed and stroked Homo, who lingered around him affectionately, and chatted with Lilybel over the remarkable adventures of their pilgrimage.

About noon Père Josef entered. His pale, thin face was sad and anxious, and his voice was full of uncertainty and trouble, as he talked in a low tone apart to Dea. "Yes, yes, my child, we must tell him. It is our duty to prepare him. They will be here in a few days."

Philip caught the words, "They will be here," and instantly his eyes were full of anxiety. "Who—who will be here?" he cried, starting up excitedly.

"*Mon enfant*, calm yourself, calm yourself," said Père Josef, laying his hand caressingly on Philip's head. "There's no cause for anxiety or inquietude. Your grandmother and uncle will be here very soon."

"Very soon," echoed Philip, despairingly. "They are coming to take me away"; and throwing himself on his pillow he burst into tears. "They are coming for me; they are coming to take me back."

"They are coming because they love you, and because you belong to them," said Père Josef, gently.

"They want to see you because you are ill. Don't excite yourself; try to be calm," urged Dea, sweetly. "No one shall take you away. Papa and I will keep you always."

"They will take me away. I belong to them. Père Josef says I belong to them. Oh, Dea, I can't go with them."

"My child, my dear boy, they do not intend to take you away," said Père Josef, greatly distressed at the boy's terror.

"Don't fret, Philip dear, don't worry; no one shall take you from us," and Dea put her arm around him protectingly.

That night Philip was restless and excited. The doctor looked grave when he came, and said decidedly that the child must sleep. "The disease has reached a point where perfect rest and sleep are absolutely necessary. Give him his composing draught, and get him to sleep as soon as possible."

Dea and Seline tried by every means to soothe and quiet him—his eyes were wide and bright, and the hot flush was again burning in his cheek. Near midnight he begged to be allowed to lie in his chair by the open window, where he watched and listened as though he were expecting some one. It was a languorous, sultry night, and the wide-open windows admitted scarcely a breath of air. At times Philip sighed and moved restlessly. Seline fanned him gently, and Dea tried to soothe him to sleep; but no, the wide-open bright eyes continued to look out into the shadows of the garden, or up to the deep blue of the sky sown with myriads of stars. Suddenly there was a faint rosy light over everything, the white flowers came out of the shadows, and the tall clusters of Easter lilies were faintly pink. The leaves shivered and shook down crystal drops, the birds twittered and called to one another across the dewy garden, the east was aglow with rose and pale opal.

"It's daylight," said Philip, softly; "I haven't slept all night. Soon the sun will rise behind the Pittosporum, just as it did when Mammy used to wake me to go to Père Josef."

"Hush, Philip, hush; try to sleep," murmured Dea, soothingly.

There was silence for a moment; then Philip suddenly started up, his eyes wider and brighter, and a smile of delight on his parted lips. "Dea, do you hear it?"

"What, Philip? What do you hear?" questioned Dea, in an awed voice.

"The Singer—he has come—I hear him! He is there, away up there, trilling, trilling," and he lifted one weak hand and pointed toward the stars growing pale in the rosy light of dawn.

Dea and Seline listened attentively, and presently they heard a distant liquid note circling nearer and nearer—the joyous morning song of a happy bird.

Philip, leaning forward, with his eyes fixed on the tiny dark object which came swiftly toward the window, uttered a feeble but sweet note which the bird evidently recognized, for it suddenly darted down to the rose-bush near the window, and there it lighted, swinging on a slender branch while it poured forth its clear, exultant song.

"It *is* the Singer, Dea," cried Philip, joyfully; "he has come back. Now I shall get well and be Toinette's Philip again."

Just then a ray of sunlight darted across the lilies, and Dea remembered that it was Easter morning. Philip leaned back on his pillow, smiling contentedly; soon the heavy lids drooped over his eyes and he was sleeping peacefully, while the bird sang on and on, joyously, exultantly; and Dea, as she listened, seemed to hear in its clear notes, "Glory to God, peace on earth, and good will toward men."

A few days after, when Madam Ainsworth and her son arrived, they found Philip much better, and quite prepared to see them. He was waiting, calm and smiling, sitting by his favorite window, his weak hand clasping Dea's as if he could borrow courage and strength from his faithful little friend. There was no one else present, and Dea never forgot that touching scene, when Madam Ainsworth, her face gentle with love and penitence, took her son's child to her heart with such affection and thankfulness that all Philip's fears and misgivings vanished instantly. With an impulse which perhaps he could not understand, he clasped her neck and whispered, "Grandmama, I love you, and I will never make you unhappy again."

These few words were all that were necessary to melt the hardest heart, and from that moment there was the most perfect understanding between them. The only other words that Dea could recall afterward were these, which were a great comfort to her. Philip had said, very gently and sweetly:

"Père Josef says you will not take me away now." And Madam Ainsworth had replied, "My darling, you shall stay here as long as you wish, and always if you prefer. From this moment I shall live to make you happy."

A few evenings after the arrival of the Ainsworths, Père Josef dropped in on a happy family group. Philip was lying in his chair under his favorite tree. His grandmama sat beside him, fanning him gently. Dea, on a low chair, was reading aloud, with Homo stretched at her feet. Mr. Ainsworth and Mr. Detrava were pacing back and forth in the rose-garden, talking earnestly— doubtless of art, for they were congenial spirits. The "children's" cage hung on a sweet-olive tree. Seline sat on the steps, sewing, and Lilybel lay curled up beside her, sound asleep.

With one glance the little priest read a happy history in the peaceful group. "*Le bon Dieu* orders everything well," he said to himself, as he stood a moment unnoticed.

When Dea saw him she laid down her book and drew a chair within the little circle.

"No, no, my child; I cannot sit. I have duties to-night which I must not be tempted to neglect. I see that all is well with you; that is enough for me."

After a few more friendly remarks he went toward the little cage where the "children" were playing merrily; and, looking at them thoughtfully for a few moments, he said, with some embarrassment and a faint flush on his thin face.

"'I SHALL LIVE TO MAKE YOU HAPPY,' SAID MADAM AINSWORTH."

"*Mon enfant*, if you don't mind, if you can spare them, I think—I think I will take the 'children' home with me to-night. You can have them whenever you wish; but to-night—well, perhaps to-night I feel a little lonely, seeing you all so happy." Sighing gently. he covered the cage with his handkerchief, and, taking it, went thoughtfully down the garden walk into the gathering twilight. Late that night, if any one had lingered near the little cottage of Père Josef, although there was not a visible ray of light, he certainly would have heard the sweet, tremulous notes of a flute softly rehearsing an old-time waltz.

Twilight gently descended on the old garden. The scent of dewy flowers filled the air. A sudden fresh gust of wind showered rose-leaves over the peaceful group. Some fell caressingly on the happy face of Toinette's Philip, and some on the bowed head of Dea while with clasped hands she murmured her evening prayer; and as they floated and fell a little brown bird clung to a slender spray and sang clearly and joyously.

CHAPTER XXXVII

A Successful Picture

I HOPE my young readers will not think I am adding an unnecessary scene to my story, if I tell them of a little incident which took place in Madam Ainsworth's drawing-room several years after the reconciliation.

In the very best light of one of the large windows stood an easel, on which a picture had just been placed. It was a simple but charming composition. The background represented an old garden—a tangle of tender green and gray—and in the center a young girl, in her first-communion veil and crown of flowers, stepped daintily down the sunlit path.

Three persons, of more or less interest to us, were gathered around the easel, examining the picture with great attention. One was Madam Ainsworth, as dignified and stately as ever, but with a much gentler expression of face, and a softer voice and manner. Near her stood a tall, slender girl with the most wonderful copper-colored hair and a wild-rose tint in her cheeks. She was not pretty, but was certainly striking, and a marked contrast to the third figure—a young girl with a lovely, delicate face and a shy, nun-like manner, whose eyes were fixed on the picture with pleased surprise.

"Dea can't criticize; she can only admire; and, Grandmama, you and Dea are very much alike in that respect," said the tall girl, in a sweet but artificial voice with a decided French accent. "Whatever Cousin Philip does is perfection. I dare say it is clever—very clever. The painters at the exhibition said so—"

"Before Philip had finished it Papa said it was remarkable for so young an artist. He worked on it while he was with us last winter," interrupted Dea, in the same soft, grave voice of her childhood.

"I'm not surprised at *your* liking it, Dea," returned the other. "Philip has made you simply angelic."

"Oh, I don't consider it a portrait," replied Dea, a faint flush coloring her delicate cheek. "It is true, Philip made a study of me for it, but he has idealized it almost beyond recognition."

"On the contrary, my dear," said Madam Ainsworth, looking fondly at the speaker, "I call it a very good likeness."

"There is certainly a likeness, and a very pretty one," exclaimed the tall girl, with a mischievous glance at Dea; "and from Grandmama's remark I see that *she* is very partial to the original."

"I'm afraid, my dear Lucille, that you don't appreciate Philip's remarkable talents as you should," said Madam Ainsworth, a little coldly.

"Indeed I do, Grandmama; I'm in a state of constant admiration. I have heard nothing but praises of that wonderful boy ever since I came home. From the eldest to the youngest in this house it is always Philip, Philip; and the utter idolatry in Bassett's eyes when he looks at him is worth coming all the way from Paris to see."

"Yes, every one loves Philip," added Dea. "Papa adores him. No one but Philip could ever induce Papa to consent to my spending a month every autumn with Madam Ainsworth; and Papa misses him so after he has made us a visit, he is hoping that when Philip leaves college he will spend his winters with us, instead of only one month."

"My dear," said Madam Ainsworth, with gentle reproof, "you forget how necessary he is to my happiness; he is so devoted, so thoughtful, really I can't be separated from him long."

"Oh, Grandmama, you have two other grandchildren," laughed Lucille. "I'm getting terribly jealous; but I like Philip immensely, and he is very nice to me, considering how badly I treated him when I was a little spoiled, selfish prig—"

Just at that moment the door was opened and Philip himself came in, eager and flushed. He held a newspaper in his hand, and his handsome face was beaming with pleasure.

"Look, Grandmama; see, Dea; listen, Cousin Lucille, while I read what they say about my picture. Uncle Edward was indignant because it was badly hung, but it has been noticed all the same. This is what they say:

"No. 270. Hung above the line, which does little credit to the discrimination of the hanging committee, etc. Tender in sentiment, truthful in drawing, with a feeling for color, and a strength and breadth not often surpassed by our best painters. We are told that the artist is only eighteen."

"Bravo!" cried Lucille, clapping her slender hands.

"It is not over-praised, my dear boy," said Madam Ainsworth, decidedly.

Dea's face expressed her happiness. When she felt most, she said least; therefore she was silent.

"Oh, it has been sent home, has it?" said Philip, glancing at the picture. "Why, it looks well in this light. You know I was so discouraged when they skied it. Now it is all right. And isn't it like Dea? That's all I value it for," he added ingenuously.

Madam Ainsworth looked at him proudly. He was such a fine, manly fellow! He had kept the beauty of his childhood, and, better than all, he had kept the simple honest nature, the frank truthful gaze, the merry laugh, and the tender loyal heart of Toinette's Philip.